LAST STAND OF THE STONE FIST
AND THE HUNTRESS

MICHAEL R. MILLER
IN ASSOCIATION WITH THE BROKEN BINDING

CONTENTS

LAST STAND OF THE STONE FIST

THE HUNTRESS

LAST STAND OF THE STONE FIST

Thank you for checking out *Last Stand of the Stone Fist*!

This novella was first written as bonus content for my mailing list alongside the launch of *Ascendant* back in September 2020. I wrote it while prepping the launch, and my timeline was squeezed, so while the novella worked well enough, I feared it lacked the polish of a full release.

Three years on, Songs of Chaos has been doing better than I could have hoped for, and while there are two more books to go in the main series, I felt it was time to divert a bit of attention to give Brode's novella the finish it deserved.

The intention of the story was to offer a little more screen time to Brode, who gave dark hints as to an interesting past, and to act as a stepping stone between books 1 and 2 of the main series. *Last Stand* is a prequel but it introduces a lot of characters and places that come to prominence in book 2 and especially book 3. All that said, it is 100% optional reading. If you only read the books, you won't miss anything, but I think anyone who enjoys this novella will find more richness in the main series. Tonally speaking, the novella acts as a bridge between *Ascendant* and *Unbound*, with darker themes from the get-go.

While my hope is people read this after finishing *Ascendant*, some might decide to read this novella first. As such, it is written with the idea in mind that someone might be coming to the world for the first time, so it doesn't go into the full depth of the magic systems for the sake of accessibility. I'll discuss the elements left out in the Afterword. Ultimately, it's a short character piece about Brode. Hopefully, you can enjoy it as that and get a kick out of seeing some of the major players of the series.

But there's more!

As a bonus, after *Last Stand*, you'll find another story of mine included in this bundle called *The Huntress* – a novella set in the world of my first trilogy, *The Dragon's Blade*. This story was originally written to be part of a free ebook anthology with a bunch of fantastic indie authors called *Lost Lore* (you can still find the collection out there). Initially, I intended to give *The Huntress* a quick polish; however, that turned into a full-blown re-write, expanding it from 11k words to a 30k-word novella. For those who have never stepped into my first trilogy, this story offers a taste of its world-building and central conflicts.

Along with *The Huntress*, this bundle also includes the world map to *The Dragon's Blade* and character concept sketches I had made by the artist David North many years ago.

I sincerely hope you enjoy both stories and look forward to hearing what you think!

Storm

Reaving River

Northern Tear

◇ Smidgar

SKARL EMPIRE

Skipta

Roaring
Fjord
◇

◇ Groef

Claw
Point
◇

Upsar
◇

FORNHEIM

Brekka
◇

FJARRHAF

Bitter
Bay

Vardguard ◇

S
◇ Sp

Sunset Sea

Stroef ◇

Haldask River

Port
Bolca
◇

RISALIA

Drakburg
◇

The Crag ◇

WITHERING
WOODS

Sidastra
◇

Red

Wismar
◇ ●

Azure

Midbell
◇

Howling Hills

FEORLEN

Toll Pass
◇

Red Rush

Range

Sable
Spire ◇ ●

Mort Morass

Versand River

BRENIN

Laone
◇

Rui
Ald

The Stretched S

S

Scalding Sea

JADE

LAKARA
◇

JU

Songs of
Chaos

WHITE WILDERNESS

hite
atch

Dead Lands

FALLOW
FRONTIER

pine

rost Fangs

Windshear
Hold

Grim Gorge

Oak Hall

COEDHEN

Brown Wash

Bright Wash

FAE FOREST

IRA

Red Rock

Loch Awe

DISPUTED
LANDS

Ruins of
Freiz

lcaer
rtress

The Serpentine

eat Chasm

MITHRAS

Alamut

Squall
Rock

ING SANDS

Negine
Sahra

AHAR

een Way

The Caged
Sea

ngkor

1

THE RETURN

Brode had hoped never to return to the Free City of Athra, much less in circumstances as dire as these. At least the means of his return were grander than those of his departure. When he had left through the Gelding Gate, he'd been only a bastard. Now he returned on the back of his beloved Erdra.

He returned as a dragon rider.

His brothers and sisters of the Order flew around him in a great wedge formation. Behind were the lower ranks, the Ascendants and Novices. At the front flew the Lords, and at their head were the Paragons, the greatest of the riders.

Brode was the rank of Champion, a hard-won accomplishment, but for many, it was the end of their advancement. If he could progress to Lord, the nature of his birth would be all but forgotten. The good people of Athra would be proud to claim him as a son of the city *then*.

Beside him flew his mentor, his sponsor, and – he hoped – his friend, Silas, riding his storm dragon Clesh. Silas gave him a reassuring nod, and Brode raised his hand in acknowledgment. In his years in the Order, Silas's support had seen Brode through far worse than painful memories.

Although it was the largest of the Free Cities, Athra seemed small from so high above. Its concentric circular walls appeared like a maze upon the plains, each ring thick and well-guarded on every point of the compass, each well-bloodied in past battles. On horseback, it was said to take a full day and night to ride around the outermost wall.

Soon, the walls would be tested again. It would be, perhaps, the greatest test they had ever faced.

The riders of Falcaer descended toward the Stallion Gate, a much grander southern entrance to the city than the gelding to the east. Both towers of the gatehouse were constructed as colossal horse heads, one painted white and the other a palomino, both luminous in the pale morning light.

Brode and his fellow Champions landed some way back from the gates, allowing the Lords and Paragons to land closest. While his brothers and sisters dismounted, Brode lingered upon Erdra's back for long enough that she reached out to him across their bond.

"All will be fine," she said, her voice as soothing in his mind as balm upon a burn.

"I know it will," he replied. *"You're here with me."*

He patted her neck, enjoying, as he often did, the glisten of her green scales like water lily leaves on a clear pond. Then he became painfully aware of how he was lingering while the other riders were already on their feet.

He jumped down and began unfastening the gear strapped to Erdra's back. Among the items was a compact chest that held his gambeson and brigandine armor.

Silas came over then, his oaken hair unaltered by their flight, but that was no surprise. After so long spent above the clouds, Silas's hair seemed caught in a permanent wind-swept state, and his skin had browned darker than any other man of Coedhen would become under the dense canopies of the forest realm.

Yet, in all other regards, he held the delicate, near-ethereal features many from the Fae Forest shared. Most striking of all were his lightning-blue eyes. Brode had once asked whether they had been that color even before bonding to Clesh, but Silas had kept that small mystery to himself.

"Do you think we'll be here long?" Brode asked in the flattened, neutral tone of Athra. "There is better work we could be doing."

"A show of our strength will bolster the resolve of the Archon." The Coedhen lilt remained strong in Silas's accent.

"I'd sooner bolster the cavalrymen the Archon will send riding to their doom. Better yet, bolster the small folk as they make their way here undefended for leagues. Better still, I'd fight the enemy."

Silas ran a spark of lightning across his knuckles. "Sometimes I wonder whether you have learned anything at all. Yet learn you shall."

"Learn what, exactly?"

"That we must sometimes play a part, as much as any courtier. This incursion will be decided here. So, it is here we must display the shine of our dragons' scales, the flash of our powers, and the sharpness of our blades."

Before Brode could reply, Silas's stony gray dragon padded over to join his rider. Clesh growled low and raked a single talon through the earth.

Silas began stroking his dragon's snout. "Clesh hungers for a fight as well." He met Brode's eye again. "We'll be flying again soon, little brother. I have no doubt."

Brode's chest swelled with pride. It always did when Silas Brightbark – third son of the esteemed family of the Free City of Coedhen – spoke to him like an equal.

From Silas's squire to fellow Champion had been a journey beyond Brode's wildest dreams. Such humble beginnings in the

Order had once been more honor than he had any right to, being born from a senator's lust, being born from chaos. Brode had a squire now in turn, the daughter of a margrave from Risalia. She and the other squires had not yet bonded to dragons of their own, so they were making the journey north from Falcaer Fortress on foot. They would pass through the villages and hamlets the riders had flown over, raising the alarm and rousing the people to head to the city.

The people will fear and worry while we dazzle the Athran senate.

Silas gave him a knowing look as if he knew that Brode still brooded on the matter.

They were spared further discussion by the opening of the Stallion Gate. Out rode what looked like half the senate upon heavy horse with billowing banners. The largest banner bore the sigil of the city – a palomino stallion's head, wreathed in the chaplet civic crown upon a red field. Senior riders gathered to meet the welcoming party.

It was all so staged.

Brode's frustration passed over his bond with Erdra. Humming, she lifted a pale green wing to envelop him.

Just then, the dragons of the Paragons – the sleek storm dragon Raiden'ra and the violet mystic dragon Wynedd – roared loud enough to be heard at the back of the flight.

Erdra lifted her head from Brode and snaked her neck to face Raiden'ra and Wynedd.

"The dragons are to rest and recover by the river north of the city."

"The Mare's Tail," Brode said. "Better to taste its waters before reaching the city, to be sure. Rest well."

Erdra lowered her head so that her snout and his forehead met. Then she took off, as did Clesh and all the others, flying high over the city.

A horn blew to summon the remaining riders into a column. Brode slung his travel sacks over his left shoulder and carried his chest of brigandine under his right arm; its weight meant little to his enhanced body. Before long, they were marching into the city, and Brode held his head high as he approached the Stallion Gate. He looked up at the looming horses' heads as he passed under them. Their long faces and huge eyes were angled down as if to judge those passing beneath. Brode wondered if these guardians of the city remembered him.

When he'd left, he'd been barely a man grown, skinny as a wheat stalk with tar-black hair and wispy fluff upon his chin. He'd filled out since then, earning his enhanced body as an Ascendant and hardening it further through battles against the scourge. Such toil may have added early grays to the black hairs, but his close-cropped beard remained dark throughout. Brode did not think the stallions would judge him a handsome man – he'd been told he had an *intense* face, whatever that meant – but he hoped they would overlook his origins and find him a worthy one.

Dutiful, daring, hardworking.

He could hope.

Soon enough, he'd passed from under the gaze of the colossal stallions and through the gate in the outermost wall. Ahead of him now lay naught but flat ground before the stronger secondary ring wall. Good earth, in truth, used for farming during the long stretches between incursions. And should the enemy breach the first wall, such good, flat ground became a killing field. On it, the horse masters of Athra could trample a horde of ghouls with ease, wheel about, take refuge through postern gates, and ride around the rings to strike the enemy again many times before inevitably falling back.

For when dealing with the scourge, you accounted for *how* you would retreat, not *if* you would. Heavy horse, great legions of armored foot, thick walls, and mighty siege engines could only slow the advance of death. Only the dragon riders could end a swarm by killing its queen; everyone else who fought did so to limit the damage as best as mortal strength could manage.

Brode and the procession of riders crossed the flat farmlands and through the gatehouse leading into the second ring. Here the bulk of Athra's horses were stabled, and an earthy smell of dung dominated the air. Row upon row of stables stretched east and west, continuing around the curvature of the walls and out of sight. An army of stable hands, trainers, smiths, and muckers tended to them amid a cacophony of neighing beasts, hammers on horseshoes, and clapping hooves.

By the time the procession passed into the third ring, human dwellings began to outnumber the stables, and the roads were paved. Inside the fourth ring, the roofs were made from red clay tiles, and mosaics adorned the footways off the main roads.

Brode appreciated these artworks more now than he had as a child. He'd taken the stonework for granted then, but in the ruined city of Aldunei – where the dragon riders kept their headquarters – the mosaics were cracked, worn by time, or else stained with the blood of countless dead. To see art and beauty again was a welcome reminder that there was a lot more to fight for.

As the riders marched through the fourth ring, people started to gather. Athrans cheered and called out thanks. Some threw golden grain before the riders as tribute, while others dropped petals. What with the mosaics, the flowers, and the many-colored weapons and armor of the riders, Brode could see how the occasion must have been splendid to behold. A grand day for all basking under an unusually warm autumn sun.

Perhaps Silas has a point. A little bolstering of their spirits will do no harm. They have enough darkness ahead.

Yet for all the beauty the city offered, Brode felt an old chill creep up his spine.

He passed a butcher's that adjoined a narrow alley, an alley down which the butcher's boy had once chased Brode before pelting him with leavings from his father's shop.

The cheers of the crowd dimmed, falling to an eerie silence. All warmth left the sun, and a whistling tune emerged from the depths of memory, pierced by the creaking twist of a leather belt. Brode laid a gentle hand upon his left forearm, where the blows still throbbed in his nightmares.

His dragon bond grew warm, and across it came Erdra's comfort and earthen strength. Brode's resolve stiffened, and he straightened his back. The phantom pain on his forearm eased. That was the past.

Brode the Bastard was now Brode the Bold.

A dragon rider.

No one could hurt him.

He gulped, and with it, the rapture of the crowd and the heat of the day returned to him in a rush. Brode raised his hand to the onlookers and smiled.

The procession carried on its winding march until at last they entered the city's fifth ring, its beating heart, where the domed roof of the senate arena dominated the skyline. A new, larger escort approached to greet the dragon riders. Both the Athran soldiers and their horses were clad in shining steel, and, after many gestures and words Brode could not hear, the Paragons continued toward the great arena while Brode and the rest were directed to an empty barrack house.

Inside, Brode and his fellow Champions took up quarters on the fourth floor. Beds for the riders stood out at intervals, covered in fine silk sheets instead of the coarser linen of the regular bunks. The Athran military, however, had not gone so far as to replace the straw mattresses with feather ones. Two of the Low Champions muttered their annoyance about that, but not Silas.

Brode chose a bed and set his travel sacks and his chest at its foot, then unstrapped his baldric, which secured the scabbard of his blade upon his back. Most riders armed themselves with a dragon steel blade, specially forged at Falcaer Fortress as a rite of passage upon reaching the rank of Ascendant. These blades were typically too long and broad to be comfortable at the waist, and Brode's was abnormally large and broad even by rider standards.

Free of his sword, he sat down, suddenly tired. A twinge ran through his soul. Erdra had not been away for long, yet he yearned for her already, as a dry throat yearns for water. Their bond was strong, perhaps too strong. He ought to be able to handle some time apart.

Yet it was hard when fleeting feelings, thoughts, and images crossed their bond from afar.

Brode saw glimpses of the dragons eating the meat gifted to them by the city. As an emerald dragon, Erdra preferred pork, even more so when covered in earthy herbs. Erdra's portion of pork had only been roasted plainly, but her pleasure still reached Brode despite the distance between them.

He pushed the sensations from Erdra aside to center himself in his actual surroundings and only noticed then that Silas had taken the bunk opposite him. Silas lay on his bed, still as stone and gazing unblinkingly at the ceiling.

What gnaws at him?

Silas had been downcast since they had lost control of the Great Chasm.

Surely he does not take that personally? We all failed.

Twenty riders led by Lord Adaskar had met the bugs pouring out of the Great Chasm, and sixteen had flown away. They had believed the surge in the scourge numbers was like any common rising from that blighted place, but the true size of this swarm had not revealed itself until the riders were well engaged. The world was about to face the largest incursion in living history, so how could a dozen Ascendants, seven Champions, and one Lord have fared better that day?

One of the fallen Ascendants had been trained as a Novice by Silas, although that had been years ago, and Silas had trained many in his time and lost no few of them. Still, something weighed on him. Something he did not wish to share with Brode.

The Champions had barely started unpacking when Lord Adaskar himself strode into their quarters. Neither especially tall nor short, Adaskar nevertheless dominated every room he was in. His skin was a dark olive hue, his hair fell in onyx waves, and his thick eyebrows framed his eyes in two great crescent moons. It all spoke of strength, right down to his brutally strong nose. But it was his spiritual presence that was the most imposing, shaking the souls of lesser riders who had enough spirit to comprehend it. It made Brode shudder, right at his very core.

"Champions," Adaskar addressed them. His voice crackled like the fire he wielded, yet even so, his Ahari tongue came through in his rhythmic, evenly paced speech. "We are to put on a martial display in the senatorial arena. Don your armor, form sparring pairs, and assemble downstairs."

He left without another look or word.

The spiritual pressure eased, lifting from Brode as though a helmet had been taken from his weary head. Already the other Champions were forming their sparring pairs.

"Silas?" Brode asked. He tried not to bother the others. Most of his brothers and sisters considered him ill luck.

"Not this time," Silas said, still staring at the ceiling. A pang went through Brode. Before he could speak, Silas went on. "We are an odd number. As the Exalted Champion present, I shall oversee the other pairs."

Relieved, Brode nodded. As an Exalted Champion, Silas was the closest among them to push at the boundaries of Lord. At best, Brode was a High Champion.

"Who shall spar with me?" Brode asked the room at large.

The response was predictable.

The two Low Champions who had scoffed at the mattress situation, Aldrich and Erna of Risalia, ignored him. Astra, who hailed from the Skarl Empire, silently joined Cateline of Brenin. Bortho of Mithras and Derec of Coedhen nodded silently across the room at each other by way of agreement.

That left one.

Ethel of Feorlen was kinder than the others. Already wearing her blue brigandine, she rolled her shoulders and strode across the barracks to him, her long blond braid swaying with each step.

"I'll knock you around a bit."

Brode got to his feet. He towered over her, but then almost everyone towered over Ethel, though they underestimated her at their peril.

"You must have forgotten our last duel," he said.

"The one where I took pity and let you win?"

Brode smirked. "As I recall, you were so out of breath you could barely yield."

"Doesn't take a mystic to conjure a convincing illusion." As Ethel passed him, she placed an icy hand upon his arm. "Bring your best this time. We're here to impress."

With that, she left.

Brode stood still for a moment, as though Ethel's powers had frozen him in place. The spot she'd touched on his forearm was the same spot still haunted by the throbs.

Unbidden, the hard creak of twisting leather rasped between his ears.

A strong hand clamped down on his shoulder, causing him to start.

"Hurry up," Silas said, then he withdrew his hand, and his booted footsteps thumped off with heavy strides.

Brode shook his head, then took out his gambeson and brigandine. The gambeson went on first, a thick quilted tunic of numerous layers of black linen that he tightened with a belt. His brigandine went on over the gambeson. This armor was composed of sheets of steel plate held together by an overlayer of hardened dark green leather. A key feature was that, unlike a full plate harness, brigandine could be put on single-handed, for its trunk strapped up the front of the torso. The vambraces went on easily; however, tightening the broad pauldrons at his shoulders occasionally gave him some trouble. After a couple of fumbles, he managed it, then strapped on his baldric so that the hilt of his sword protruded high above his right shoulder. Clad in his green brigandine and with the reassuring weight of his great sword, Brode always felt much more the part.

Now ready, he hurried out to follow Silas, Ethel, and the others.

2

MATTERS OF CONCERN

The senatorial arena of Athra turned out to be the largest paddock Brode had ever seen, ringed at ground level by a red fence the height of a man and surrounded by elevated tiers of seating. The Archon's box loomed in pride of place, yet the Archon himself was nowhere to be seen – doubtless he was off with the Paragons to discuss the incursion instead.

Despite growing up in the city as the son of a senator, Brode had never set foot inside the arena before. His true father wanted him kept away, kept hidden. Yet Brode had heard tales of the senators making their speeches on horseback, their arguments judged as much by their riding skill as by the strength of their words.

Today, it was the riders of Falcaer who took up the arena floor, while Athra's elite watched from on high. These equestrians wore silk or velvet riding jackets over shirts with oversized white cuffs rolled up from the wrist. Cream woolen breeches and high leather boots completed their attire.

As Brode scanned their faces, his gut squirmed. Fearing he would soon see his father, he braced for the pang. Was he looking down upon the arena, trying to find Brode in turn? Unlikely. Tense as a coiled snake, Brode searched and searched but could not find his father anywhere in the stands.

Perhaps he was no longer sitting on those benches and Brode's half-brother Carlo had taken over the family duty. After Brode moved to Falcaer Fortress, he had not received news of them, and he had not desired to ask. Dragon riders left their past behind. Now, his only brothers and sisters were in the Order.

The call rang out to begin, and Brode dropped his eyes back to the arena floor and met Ethel's cold eyes, though her gaze was warm. He bowed to her. She returned the courtesy, then drew her sword. Its steel was pale blue, long and flowing to a fine tip like an icicle. She handed it to him expectantly.

Taking her sword, Brode looked inward. Given the distance between him and Erdra, her core appeared diminished through the window of their soul-bond. When they were close, her core looked like a great mountain, but at present, it looked more like a grassy knoll. Drawing magic at such a distance was unpleasant, but Brode managed to draw on a small portion, and he wove the power of the earth along Ethel's blade to blunt it. A necessary precaution. One mistake or over-eager strike with dragon steel and not even the toughened bodies of a Paragon would deflect the cut. Other riders could blunt weapons in their own manner, but Brode's technique was especially effective.

He tossed Ethel's sword back to her, then drew his own broad green blade. Rather than a tip, the steel ended in a slanted edge, which scraped the ground as he held it at his side. He blunted his blade as well, and then they began.

Throughout the arena, riders displayed their skills with sword, mace, spear, and a little magic sprinkled in for show. Thick dust flew up from the dry floor. Steel sang, and magical techniques cracked and banged as they collided.

Ethel won their first bout by icing the floor underfoot, causing

Brode to slip. The second he won, and the third dragged out until they battled into the path of another pairing, at which point Silas ordered them to reset.

Breathing hard, Brode noticed people were circling the arena at ground level. They must have been on horseback, but as the dividing fence hid the horses from view, it created a strange effect of Athrans floating along upon thin air, goggling at the riders as though they were prized animals in a menagerie.

Put on display indeed, Brode thought.

These new onlookers were not noble. There were mothers sharing a saddle with their children, skinny boys with awe in their eyes, rank-and-file horsemen of the regular cavalry, matrons, maids, and plump merchants tossing a few coins to the duelers. This time, Brode scanned for his mother, but she wasn't there either.

"Shall we go again, then?" Ethel called.

Brode entered a guard position, holding his sword at head height and tilting his blade toward the ground. When Ethel came at him, her strokes were as precise as they were quick. Even by Champion standards, she was fast. To the onlookers, their blades might have appeared as flashes of color. Brode remained steadfast, blocking each of her blows. Erdra's earthen magic had made him defensive by nature, waiting to exploit a foe's mistake.

The issue was Ethel hardly made any, at least during a real spar. Here, on show, they added acrobatics and whirling spins, the sort of pointless flourishes that would result in death when fighting an abomination or a flayer but which delighted the crowd. And which caused Ethel to overreach, meaning Brode scored as many wins as losses as the day wore on.

In time, their score stood at five rounds apiece. During the eleventh clash, a sudden swell of joy crossed his dragon bond, and Erdra's core grew larger in his mind's eye. Brode paid for that moment of distraction. Ethel struck his calf, side-stepped his clumsy counter, then found his waist. Pain seared in his hip bone, and he sank to his knee.

Ethel offered him a hand, which he gladly took.

Silas passed them, telling the Champions to end on a high note. With the dragons returning, the show must be nearing its end.

Brode caught Ethel's eye, raised his left hand, and mouthed the word 'shield' to her. After a moment, she understood his meaning.

They engaged. After clashing blades three times, they theatrically parted, and then Ethel played her part. White-blue power formed around her left arm until she released her Shard ability: a jagged lump of freezing cold that she sent hurtling toward him.

Simultaneously, Brode drew on Erdra's magic. His dragon bond flared hot, power entered his body through his soul, then he channeled it down his left arm and a square shield of stone emerged from his hand. Even for him, the weight was too great without the assistance of further magic, but raise it he did, and Ethel's Shard shattered against the rock.

The nearby crowd began clapping. A brief twinge ran through Brode's heart. Hearing the applause was... gratifying. That surprised him. It shouldn't have been. Such a small measure of appreciation shouldn't have pleased him so much. But it did.

An idea came to him. One to make the crowd really go wild.

The other riders were already bowing to each other and sheathing their weapons, but Brode caught Ethel's eye again. He let his rock shield fall to the ground, then opened and clenched his left hand into a fist.

This time, she frowned. Her look seemed to say, 'you're not ready,' but Brode kept opening and clenching his fist and worked his face into what he hoped was a confident expression. It would be fine. Her sword was blunted, so she could not do him any real damage.

Ethel hesitated, then rushed forward and thrust her sword toward him, her natural strength enough to send a bull reeling back.

Brode channeled fresh magic down his left arm and summoned some of his burgeoning spiritual strength to *will* the power to form as he desired. A second skin of stone wove into being over his hand and forearm, and he moved to catch Ethel's blade in his armored hand. The edge of her blue blade met his rock-coated skin with a spine-shuddering crack.

That gained a good deal of attention. The applause drew the attention of yet more Athrans. A child in his mother's saddle pointed and whooped in high-pitched glee, and at least one aghast citizen almost fell from his horse.

His heart racing, Brode tried to go further and bend his fingers to grip the blue steel and wrest it from Ethel's control. Two fingers closed over the blade, but no more. As adept as he had become with the technique, he still lacked full flexibility. In time, he hoped to be able to form a stony brigandine over himself and thus provide the ultimate form of defense against the pincers, fangs, and claws of the scourge.

"What are you doing?" Ethel said, concerned. "Let go."

With an effort, he unfurled his fingers enough so she could withdraw her sword. Only then did he feel the sharp pain in his hand and notice the steady trickle of dark blood falling to the dusty earth.

Ethel was by his side in a moment, her sword sheathed. "I told you," she chided, pulling his hand down. "Let me see."

The stone skin began to break apart, the pieces sliding off as though slickened by a film of oil. His palm had suffered a cut across its full width, and the flesh around it had been bruised black. A few tiny fragments of sharp stone were embedded in his hand like thorns.

Ethel ran her thumb gently around the wound. He winced, but as she continued, the pain ebbed away.

"What's happened here?"

Silas's voice cut through Brode like a boom of his thunderous power.

Brode gulped, then Silas was upon them. He glanced between Brode's injured hand, the stone on the ground, and Ethel tending to him, then his eyes narrowed. Ethel let go at once and stepped back.

Silas cleared his throat, then spoke to Brode. "As ever, your boldness gets the better of you." He bent to pick up one of the stone pieces, holding it between finger and thumb. "The will behind it is already dissipating. Doubtless that was why it cracked. Be mindful not to attempt this in battle. One slip against a flayer—"

"And I'll be Brode the 'Stone Stump'."

Ethel smiled, amused.

Silas looked anything but amused. "You must keep meditating on your spiritual development as a priority."

Brode might have said such things were easier said than done, which was true, and he might have said that reflecting upon inner truths was hard when a battle with a scourge swarm was so near – also true – but it was neither the time nor the place, and they'd been over the lessons half a hundred times already. Expanding one's soul to grow one's spiritual strength was simply *challenging*. It was what separated High Champions from Exalted Ones, and it was what kept many riders from advancing to the rank of Lord or Lady. It was what took freshly made Lords from the lowest tiers to the dizzying heights of a Paragon.

In the end, Brode simply said, "I will endeavor to advance, Master Brightbark."

Silas looked over his shoulder. "If there is nothing more, Champion Ethel, you're dismissed."

"Yes, Master Brightbark." She bowed, gave Brode an apologetic look, and then headed to join Cateline of Brenin in conversation.

Silas threw Ethel a measured look, then said quietly, "I thought we discussed this matter already."

"There's nothing of concern."

Silas met his eye. "I've always stood up for you. Please don't let me down."

Brode's throat went dry. "I won't."

But Silas was no longer paying attention to Brode; rather, he had craned his neck as though to gaze through the domed roof. Seconds later, the first roar of the returning dragons reached Brode's ears.

"*Is something wrong?*" Erdra asked. "*You feel tense.*"

"*It's nothing. How was your meal?*"

"*Rejuvenating. It had been too long since I heard a flowing river and felt the grass beneath my talons.*"

Brode felt such a swell of joy at her return he felt compelled to say, "*I missed you.*"

"*Hmm,*" Erdra hummed, half in amusement and half in concern. "*I missed you too, my hermit.*" Across their bond, she sent him the impression of a tilled field between two great walls. "*Find me here after your own feast.*"

"*Feast?*" Brode asked, but before Erdra could answer, the crackling voice of Lord Adaskar called.

"Form ranks!"

The Athran crowds, whether common citizens or noble equestrians, were dispersing.

The show was over.

Brode fell into line beside Silas as the dragon riders began marching toward a palatial-sized door on the arena floor. He wished to ask with a bite, 'Are we to impress the Archon with the size of our appetites too?' but he refrained. A bastard learned to hold their tongue, as a rider also did.

But Silas knew him too well. "Try to enjoy it, little brother."

Brode nodded with a grunt.

"Remember what we face," Silas said.

A writhing dark mass, enough to swallow the sun. A buzzing horde of living poison, of screeching death, ready to sweep across the world and leave all living things blackened and decayed.

"How could I forget?"

"Then you'll recall how some did not make it back. Enjoy tonight and tomorrow as well. Each day left is precious."

Brode frowned but dutifully nodded again. He would smile, he would wave, he would stand, he would hold, he would be the first strike and the last shield. He would even put on a show, apparently. He would do whatever duty the Order desired.

3

A TASTELESS FEAST

The feasting hall's floor was one great mosaic depicting a herd of colorful horses as varied as the dragons of the Order. A twinkle reflected off each bright exposed tile.

While Brode was pleased to be sitting beside Silas, he was unfortunately sitting opposite Aldrich, who complained about the lack of cushions. As far as Brode was concerned, Aldrich should have stayed in his comfortable life as a margrave in Risalia. What with his insufferable conversation and Silas's dour mood, Brode did not enjoy much of the evening and found his attention wandering around the hall.

Riders sat with members of their rank. The Novices sat closest to the door. One table up were the Ascendants, who comprised the bulk of their number. After the Champions' table sat the three Lords present, Adaskar first among them, while the two Paragons sat at the high table along with the senators and Archon.

There sat Vald, Paragon of Storms. The air around him seemed fraught, crackling with power. And beside him was Eso, Paragon of Mystics, whose eyes always seemed to look through you, into you, anywhere but strictly at you. The other esteemed Paragons had been far from Falcaer when the turmoil began, though they would already be on their way. It was said that Eso and his dragon Wynedd could enter a trance and communicate with the other Paragons across the whole world if need be.

Sitting on either side of the Paragons and looking diminutive by comparison were half a dozen senators from Athra. Brode scanned their faces, his heartbeat picking up again, fearing who he might find. Once more, he was able to breathe a sigh of relief. He recognized none of them, including the Archon. Twenty years of absence would do that, he supposed.

Little distinguished the Archon from his fellow senators – a wine-red velvet riding jacket, cream-colored breeches, and fine brown leather boots. Yet, as the first amongst equals, the Archon was entitled to wear the civic crown: a chaplet of hay, leaves, and fruit-bearing branches woven around a horseshoe band of iron.

The Archon of Athra stood. As he addressed the gathering, a small army of kitchenhands and maids entered from the side doors of the hall. They carried platters and dishes laden with the finest fare of Athra. A roast boar became the centerpiece of each table, accompanied by turnips, lettuce, and radishes. Bowls heaped with olives – green, black, and stuffed with goat cheese – were set beside wooden boards piled with steaming white loaves and deep dipping dishes of oil and vinegar. No wine was served. It would take quantities deadly for regular humans to leave a tingle in the fingers of the Lords and Paragons, and the good senators would not wish to become drunk while their guests maintained their wits.

Brode reached for an olive bowl and caught a glimpse of one of the maids approaching the Champions' table.

His gut twisted.

The pang he had been bracing for struck, only it wasn't for his father or stepfather.

She was slight, with a sinewy frame from years of labor. Frayed ends plagued her black hair, now rapidly draining of color, and her eyes were haunted and gray. His mother's fortieth year had only just passed, but she looked far older.

Brode's shock, anxiety, and even fear boiled so hot and fierce that it spilled over his bond with Erdra.

"Who troubles you, my hermit? To whom must I teach a lesson?"

"She's here."

Brode had frozen midway while reaching across the table for the olives.

Such behavior drew attention to him. His mother caught on, turning to see what all the Champions were looking at.

Their eyes met. His heart thumped painfully. Her arms trembled, then she dropped the jug of oil she'd been holding. At the end of the Champions' table, Bortho caught the jug and handed it back to her without taking his eyes from his food.

Beside Brode, Aldrich uttered a haughty snort. "Careful, woman," he called through a mouthful of boar. And then, in a lower tone, he turned to Silas and Brode and said, "What's become of the standards in Athra? No self-respecting margrave or land-grave would ever allow someone that decrepit to serve visiting riders."

Brode almost stood up, but Erdra sent a pulse that weighed him down.

His mother made hurried apologies, bobbing her head in a series of bows as she withdrew herself from the Champions table.

Brode's feet and hands felt leaden. He couldn't move, though whether that was Edra's magic or his own shock, he couldn't say.

His heart continued to thunder as he noticed his mother favoring one side and how the sleeves of her tunic were drawn tight at her wrists while the other kitchenhands had theirs rolled up against the heat.

Sat with arms spread and staring grimly off into the distance, his food untouched, Brode once again earned Aldrich's attention.

"Are you touched in the head?" He shoved the bowl of olives to Brode's side. "Eat something already."

At last, Brode unfroze. He flexed his fingers and curled his toes. Now his appetite had vanished, and without meaning to, he clutched at his left forearm.

Silas gave him an inscrutable look.

Brode wondered if he knew. He must do. The question was whether he would understand.

As he picked mechanically at some bread and olives, other feelings began to rise, ones he had not been expecting. Regret, longing, and something else. Not quite love, not exactly. It might have been pity.

Were they his feelings or Erdra's? Sometimes, it could be hard to tell. Her tender heart flitted into him more and more as the years wore on. Power and magic flowed one way through the bond, after all. The dragon seeps into the human.

"*Should I do something?*" he asked Erdra.

"*You shouldn't do anything.*" Her words said one thing, her tone the other. "*What do you want to do?*"

Chewing – and indeed doing anything else while mentally communicating with one's dragon – wasn't the easiest or most comfortable sensation, but it allowed him to speak with Erdra without anyone suspecting that the feast wasn't his sole focus.

"*I have no mother,*" Brode said. "*Not since I swore the oath. No father, no blighted stepfather or half-brother. You're right. I ought to do nothing. But—*"

Somehow, for the first time, he thought about that 'but'. In matters concerning Ethel, he'd always been able to push his emotions down no matter how hard, but in this?

"*I'll go to her.*"

When Erdra did not answer, he assumed she disapproved.

"*Erdra?*"

"*I won't tell,*" she said, though it was plain she was as conflicted as him.

The real trouble would be in sneaking away from the others.

And so the feast went tastelessly on. The Archon bleated about the great role the riders would play in the coming conflict and how the city's cavalry would ride the harder for their presence. Vald, Paragon of Storms, thanked the Archon and the good senators and humbly accepted the tasks laid before them. The Mystic Paragon, Eso, spoke next, though his cryptic words were likely to cause the senators a headache to puzzle out.

As honey cakes and fruit platters were being served, Brode strained to see his mother at the far end of the hall by the Novices' table. Ethel caught him in the act and gave him a concerned look from across the length of the Champions' table. He feigned disappointment, mouthing 'figs' and giving a shiver, but such a feeble story did not satisfy her. Frowning, she gave him a reproachful look before Astra and Derec pulled her back into their conversation.

After the last of the dishes were cleared away and the final speech of the Archon had been made, the Paragons ordered the riders outside to Cleanse and Forge throughout the night to make up for lost time that day. That gave Brode an opening. If nobody was expected to be back in the barracks until morning, he had an opportunity.

The riders began leaving the hall, the Paragons first, then the Lords, and so on. Each type of rider would go off in search of suitable locations for their meditations. While Cleansing a dragon's core only required proximity, Forging additional raw motes of magic into the core was another matter.

Silas and the other storm riders Forged most effectively when amidst heavy weather. When the wind was still, as this night was, they might Forge on the backs of their dragons as they flew. As an ice rider, Ethel would doubtless descend to some cold, dark cellar. The fire riders had it easy, for a brazier could always be lit. The mystics drew upon energy from the thoughts of others, so a city like this offered a veritable bounty of mystic motes.

Brode had a middling level of difficulty in finding motes to Forge into Erdra's core. Emerald dragons were attuned to nature. Some were connected best to plants and the living world, and some, like Erdra, were connected to the earth. It meant there was always somewhere close by Brode could meditate, but that didn't make it easy. Rock and earth held onto their power as stubbornly as mountains fought the decay of time.

Earlier, Erdra had shown him that she was resting in one of the open, recently tilled fields in the outer ring of the city to the north. That was where he should have gone after leaving the feast. Brode headed east instead.

He did not make it far before Silas caught him. His mentor pulled him into a dark recess beside a luxury saddle shop and held him in place.

"Erdra isn't that way." Clesh must have known where she was and told Silas. "Where are you going, little brother?"

"To right a wrong."

Silas's expression was grave, but he held Brode firmly in place. "Our pasts do not matter. Not after we swore the oath."

"Then they should take our memories away."

"Don't go," Silas urged.

"Is that an order?"

A part of him yearned for the order, for the scolding of a superior to stop him. Following an order would be much easier. Choosing not to go, choosing to look the other way, doing nothing – and so upholding his oath – that would be harder.

"I just... need to speak with her."

Silas wrinkled his nose and grunted powerfully enough to be a dragon. "Don't let me down," he said, then, slowly, he let Brode go. "I seem to have lost track of you in the alleyways."

Erdra voiced her surprise. *"He's letting you go?"*

"Best not to question it."

Not wishing to give Silas time to change his mind, Brode nodded, said his thanks, and then set off at a run.

4

MOTHER

Brode sped cat-like through the darkening city. With a curfew now in place, few civilians remained out after dark, and the soldiers and watchmen would not question a rider.

He made it to the crammed easternmost streets of the third ring in good time, then slowed his pace. Each step became somehow heavier. He had wandered these streets so often as a lad, but they seemed so small and narrow to him now. Perhaps that was a natural part of growing up, seeing the places he once had for their true size, or perhaps he was simply no longer afraid like he'd been as a child?

Despite his Champion's body, his heart thumped painfully hard. He wasn't out of breath. So, no, he had to admit he wasn't entirely free of the fear. Not for himself, at any rate.

At last, he came within sight of his old home – a five-story insula block built of thin red bricks like countless others in the third ring. Wedged between two other insula blocks, all that distinguished Brode's one was the water well situated outside. The higher floors of each insula were made of timber, making them less spacious than the lower levels, and Brode's old abode was on the top floor.

He approached quietly and carefully, ducking into the cramped alley between his old building and its neighbor. Squatting, Brode pressed one palm against the ground and another against the wall of his building. As his connection with Erdra had grown stronger, he had found he could comprehend vibrations through rock and stone, as though the earth had a language of its own.

While not yet a master of this technique, he could register four people on the first floor sitting around a fire and a heavyset person pacing two floors up. Straining to discern the fifth floor, he managed to register two people walking up there. His mother and someone with an awkward gait. He did not recall his stepfather having a limp, although a pained limp would be all Kuret Watcher deserved.

Brode considered entering, climbing the stairs, breaking down his old front door, and confronting the man head-on – to see the fear flicker behind Kuret's eyes.

He withdrew his hand from the wall and shook his head in an attempt to clear it. For all he knew, the limping person wasn't Kuret at all. Kuret might have died, and his mother might have found someone new. Gathering himself, he waited instead. If it was Kuret, then coming face to face with his stepfather would doubt-less drive away whatever sense remained in him. And Brode wasn't even sure what his goal was in coming here, only that he felt compelled to know whether Kuret had been up to his old ways.

He remained crouched in the alley until night truly fell, the sky turning ink-dark and clouded. If it was Kuret, he'd leave for his shift on patrol soon. Taking a deep breath, Brode placed his hand back against the wall. Sure enough, the heavier set of feet on the fifth floor made awkwardly for the door. He tracked the vibrations as the same person tackled the flights of stairs slowly, following them all the way until the front door of the building opened and a man walked out with laboring breaths.

Crouched in the alley, Brode could not see him, not even his back. The man heaved, hawked spit, then closed the door with a bang. Brode remained in the shadows as the man shuffled into sight. A cloak hid most of his frame, and the lantern he held did not emit enough light to illuminate his features, but Brode was certain it was him. Kuret had once seemed a giant to Brode, yet now he looked so old. His limp and hunched shoulders diminished what little size and strength remained to him.

An urge came upon Brode to seize him, to throw his full, enhanced strength into a backhanded blow just like Kuret favored.

Yet the moment passed. Brode remained crouched in the shadows. Kuret uttered a groan, stretched, and then began marching into the night, whistling a light tune.

At once, the old chill shot up Brode's spine, and he relived the flashes of panic cowering behind doors as the whistling drew closer. His fingers twitched, but Erdra's presence rushed over their bond once more to stay his hand.

"We're here to protect, to defend."

Brode let loose a shuddering sigh. Gulping, he removed his hands from the stones and let Kuret hobble away into the night, his lantern swaying in time to his music.

Once the watchman was long gone, Brode dusted off his palms, then edged out of the alley and entered the insula. The hallway within was cold and dark. He found it suffocating. The stairs loomed over him, sloped and steep as a sheer cliff. When he reached his old door, he stopped again.

Raised a fist.

Lowered it.

At last, he knocked.

"Kureee?" his mother cooed. "Have you forgotten something?"

That sent a twinge through Brode. She sounded... *happy?* That could not be right.

Footsteps pattered closer, and then the door opened wide. His mother stood in the doorway, her features changing as she drank in her visitor. Her smile turned to an expression of confusion, then fear, then shock. She backed away.

"Brode?"

"Mother," he struggled to say. "May I come in?"

Her mouth trembled wordlessly, but she managed to nod.

Brode stepped in, feeling more nervous than he'd been before his first battle with the scourge. As with so many things in the third ring of Athra, this place felt miniscule – and even smaller than he recalled. A squat kitchen, table, and bed behind a curtain. *No wonder we always felt on top of each other.* A draft still crept in through the windowsill, undoing the work of the tiny fireplace.

"I shouldn't be here, but—"

"You shouldn't." She backed farther away as though he had the blight in him. As her back touched the wall, she winced and clutched at her side, the same side she'd been favoring during the feast.

Brode's heart skipped a beat. He'd let Kuret walk free tonight, but if he found proof of fresh injuries after all this time, not even Erdra could hold him back.

He finally took a step toward her. "Mother—"

She threw out one arm to stay him, folding the other over her chest.

Brode halted. "I... I saw you serving at the feast."

"I know," she said, unable to meet his eye. "I didn't have a choice but to be there—" She cut herself off. Stared at the floor. "Kuret... isn't here."

"I know."

She finally looked at him. "Are you going to hurt him?"

Brode swallowed hard. "I'm not sure."

"They said you'd become a real rider. They said that meant you weren't supposed to come back or have a family no more."

"Mother," he said, fiercer now. "Has he been hurting you?"

She blinked as though she didn't comprehend. "Oh no, no... that's all in the past. Been years and years since, and he never—"

"Mother!" Brode fought to contain his voice. His bond with Erdra flared hot and bright, but he pushed on. "You can tell me."

"There's nothing to tell."

"You're favoring one side. You're obviously hurt."

"That wasn't Kuret, though!" For the first time, she had energy about her. "It wasn't. I fell."

It took all his effort and a fresh, soothing wave from Erdra for Brode not to scream.

"You cannot expect me to believe that."

"But it's true. I was heading out to fetch water a few weeks back, and it was raining, and I fell. Slipped on the mud by the well and thumped me ribs on the wall. Nearly fell in, I did. I screamed, and Kuret came running down, still half-dressed, getting ready for his patrol. Honest. Go downstairs and ask old Mrs. Fuller – she'll tell you the same."

Brode was tempted, if only to check whether Kuret had been threatening the old laundress too. And yet something about his mother's plea gave him pause. She had never defended him so vehemently before.

"Will you show me your arms?"

"What?"

"Your arms, Mother. Roll up your sleeves."

From the look on her face, he might have asked her to strip naked. With shaking fingers, she began unlacing the sleeves of her gown at the wrist. As she rolled up her right sleeve, Brode's heart skipped another beat.

There was nothing. No signs of hurt at all.

"And the other?"

Something was not right. Brode touched his own left arm as she rolled up her left sleeve. Once more, she revealed unblemished skin.

"It's fine." She spoke with pity in her voice now, and such a tone made him feel worse than ever. "There's nothing wrong,

Brode. It's been much better, so much better since... since you left."

Her words did not quite register with him.

"But the other kitchenhands, the maids – their sleeves were up."

"I'm getting old, boy. You think I want to be sweating all over those fine riders? Don't need no harsh words from them if I can help it. Got some anyways in the end, didn't I?"

"But..." Brode was lost. "Why," he said, seizing on a new point of attack, "why would they make you work if you're injured?"

She looked him up and down. "Have you forgotten what it's like to live here and not at your fancy rider palaces?" She shook her head before he could answer. "You should go."

Brode stepped forward.

Her back still against the wall and unable to retreat farther, his mother shrank into herself.

"You look so worn," he said.

"Thought you'd be an' all. Don't they work you hard, them riders? Or is it all feasting?"

"We train endlessly. We protect you and everyone."

"Do you? What are all those walls and soldiers for then? Meager pay enough we get, then the rider tithes come along and take some more. Seems like you're a lot of nobles playing with your magic."

This set a fire under her. Talk of nobles always did.

"Don't come back after all this time like it's so important to you. Your wretched father was at least shamed into teaching you to read and write and speak proper. Got your sword training, too. D'you know what that was like for Kuret? You coming back here those nights with a hot meal in your belly and good new boots while his belly rumbled and his boots wore through."

"How can you defend him?" Brode pulled up his own sleeve to show her his arm – the left one, the one he'd raised to deflect Kuret Watcher's belt. The scars had healed since he'd gained an enhanced body, but he showed her all the same. As he'd done half a hundred times as a child. "He did it to you, too!"

"Only when I tried to stop him," she said, and she had the grace to look ashamed that she hadn't intervened on every occasion. "Those were just mistakes, though. He didn't mean it. He cried sometimes, you know."

Brode began rocking on the balls of his feet, his mind now a storm of confusion and grief.

Why did I come here?

Heat prickled along his nose and into the corners of his eyes. For the first time since leaving his home, he had to fight back tears.

Children cry, not grown men with beards. Not a Champion.

"Erdra?" he gasped, his internal voice mimicking his physical state. But his emotions were now in such disarray he couldn't focus on the bond well enough to reach her.

He was alone again.

Lost.

Just as he'd been before he'd left this room.

Seeing her son in distress at last awakened something primal in Pavi Maid. She reached out a trembling hand and patted Brode's own.

"You were so young," she said softly. "You won't remember what it was like for us. What they called me. What they called you."

Oh, but he did remember.

"Chaos bringer," Brode muttered.

There had been far worse names, of course. He also recalled what his old tutor had said when teaching him and his half-brother their letters. That he was fortunate to have senatorial blood in his veins, for other bastards would not be so fortunate.

He called me lucky…

His mother carried on as though he had not spoken. "And Kuret and I had been so happy before… before—"

"That wasn't your fault." He sniffed, but the tears did not fall. He had the strength to keep them at bay.

"No, no, it weren't," she said, as though recalling it from another life. For all the world, it might as well have been another life. "But it happened. Kuret could've been better about it – that he could've, but it's done now. It's done." She nodded with an air of finality. "I weren't ready for a child at sixteen, never mind one like you. I'm glad to see you so strong and well, but... you should go. It's for the best."

She gave his hand one final pat, then withdrew hers.

For a moment, Brode might have turned to leave. And this time, it definitely wasn't from Erdra's power. He didn't so much as twitch.

He had been a fool to come. What had driven him here? If pressed, he would have said it was love, or what twisted thing he considered love – the lingering dependency of a small, scared child. Whatever this feeling was in him, it was the closest thing to love that he'd ever felt for another person.

And now he'd discovered that those feelings had been founded on sand. To Pavi Maid, Brode was only a reminder of the calamity that had befallen her and many more terrible things thereafter. Living proof of her misery. Everyone had been better off once he'd left. His presence now only threatened to reignite old flames. He was as unwanted here as when he'd first arrived at Falcaer Fortress, which was only right, fair, and proper.

How could chaos bringers like him be welcomed anywhere?

With a great effort, he managed to speak. "I'm sorry," he croaked. He lingered for what felt a terribly long time. Somehow, he couldn't escape the strange feeling that while everything else about his old life had seemed small and unthreatening, his mother now towered over him.

At last, his strength gave out.

He turned on his heel and fled.

5

NOWHERE

Two days passed, and the Paragons concluded their plans with the masters of Athra. The riders were summoned to assemble in the training ground of their barracks, and Brode now stood at attention with the other Champions, fully armored and ready to take the fight to the scourge.

With the Paragons busy, it fell again to Lord Adaskar to handle the rank and file. He strode up and down the riders, addressing them as a general might an army.

"Riders of Falcaer," he called in his crackling voice. "The Archon and his senators have wisely taken our advice. This great swarm will be encouraged toward Athra, where we shall break it or else die in the attempt. At day's end, messengers will ride from every gate to raise the summons and seek aid from every power, from Smidgar in the north to Lakara in the south and from Sidastra in the west to Negine Sahra in the east."

Though Lord Adaskar was an Ahari by birth, he showed no special pride in mentioning Negine Sahra, his people's jewel of a city. Lord Adaskar took his oath seriously.

"The world will come together as one," he continued, "and we will prevail. Yet until the swarm is brought to these walls, there is cause for concern. There is a risk that the swarm will splinter and veer toward Mithras or Coedhen, or both. We must ensure that does not happen."

Brode nodded along. Scourge swarms were naturally drawn to the densest population nearby. The complication here was that the swarm had emerged from the eastern edge of the Great Chasm, almost as close to the city of Mithras as it was to Athra. The summons had already gone out into Athra's sphere of influence, meaning a great deal of people would be heading to the city, into harm's way, for the very purpose of luring the swarm where the riders wanted it. A grim necessity that none took lightly. 'As serious as a summons' was a common phrase among the people of every nation in the world.

Some of Mithras's outer settlements would also have to be evacuated for safety, but if the population of the island city swelled too high in turn, then some of the swarm might be pulled south and east rather than west to Athra.

It was a delicate matter to get right.

Adaskar finished pacing. "Every rider must perform exceptionally, else we will fail before the true battle begins. Novices, you shall fly to alert every Order Hall from here to the Skarl Empire."

A few of the Champions exchanged looks at that. Summoning riders from subordinate regional Order Halls was not lightly done. On occasion, the scourge would rise in multiple places at once, so leaving any region without its full complement of dragon riders was tantamount to desperation.

Fresh smoke escaped Adaskar's lips. "Ascendants, you shall fly to settlements within Athra's territory and help guard the columns destined for the city. Champions, you shall be split into teams led by a Lord or Lady to harry the enemy."

Lord Adaskar clicked his fingers. Rolekeepers of Athra carrying bundles of paper scurried in beside him, then followed as Adaskar began handing out the orders to the riders, starting with the Novices.

While there was still time, Brode turned to Silas. They hadn't spoken much since Brode had confronted his mother, and Silas hadn't enquired about Pavi, Kuret, or any of that sordid business. Silas had seemed satisfied enough that Brode had returned without incident.

Brode was grateful for his trust but found the continued silence worrisome. Silas's mood had not improved during their time in the city. If anything, his dourness had grown into a darkness, as though one of his own storm clouds enveloped his heart.

"It will be good to get back out there," Brode said. "Good to get away. I feel ready," he added, as if already marching to his death.

Silas eyed him. "None of us are."

Despite Brode's eagerness, Silas's words shook him. "You're as close as any Champion can be to the rank of Lord. If we make it through this—"

"Then it will all come around again, little brother." He sounded bone tired. "Maybe I'll be a Lord or even a Paragon, but it will all happen again."

Before Brode could say anything further, Lord Adaskar reached the Champions.

"You shall be split into strike teams. Aldrich, Erna, Bortho, Astra, report to Paragon Vald. Everyone else, report to Paragon Eso."

Brode had not even taken a step when Adaskar caught his arm, and he had to restrain himself from wincing from the heat in the Fire Lord's hand.

"Champion Brode, a moment."

"How can I assist you, Master Adaskar?"

"I have need of you elsewhere." Adaskar presented Brode with a scroll. "Your orders."

The wax on the parchment bore the rearing stallion seal of the Archon of Athra. That struck Brode as odd. Riders were apart from politics and any government. Only riders commanded riders, but then his mind caught up. In times like these, riders could be granted the power to order the summons and to requisition supplies as needed. The Novices and Ascendants would have received missives giving them such authority from the Archon to assist in readying the city for the siege, but why was he, a Champion, being handed it?

Breaking the seal, Brode unfurled the scroll and scanned the words. He did so twice to be sure, but alas, he had not read them wrong. He was to fly east to the Disputed Lands and manage evacuations there as required.

"Forgive me, Master Adaskar, but should I not also join a strike team?"

"Are you questioning the wisdom of the Paragons?"

Brode considered his response carefully. He had a horrible feeling about what the real reason behind this was.

"Is there a problem, Master Adaskar?"

Silas had doubled back to join them. When he noticed the scroll in Brode's hand, he quickly scanned it, eyes darting back and forth, then pressed his mouth into a thin line.

Adaskar exhaled more smoke. "Champion Silas, do you question the wisdom of the Paragons as well?"

Silas met the Lord eye-to-eye. "Brode is a Champion. He should fly with us."

Brode felt both elated that Silas had come to his defense and sickened at the thought of the consequences of such clear insubordination.

Adaskar glanced at Brode again. He wrinkled his nose as though smelling the taint of chaos. When he spoke again, he spoke to Silas. "As you will, Brightbark. You will join Champion Brode on his errand."

A spark of silver power flashed in Silas's eye. "You cannot be serious—"

It happened in a split second. Lord Adaskar only began gathering his spiritual power, but its sheer force seemed to have a physical weight, pressing down on Brode's soul, and he wasn't even the intended target.

Silas's cheek twitched, but he averted his eyes and said no more.

The pressure eased. Brode breathed easily again and inclined his head. "We will not fail you, Master Adaskar."

"See you do not." Adaskar swept back to address the riders at large. "You will all face decisions too terrible to contemplate, yet make them you must. What is our first lesson?"

"We cannot save them all," the riders chanted back.

Lesson one. The hardest one. It had always left a bitter taste in Brode's mouth.

"Return before a moon's turn," Lord Adaskar said. "Cleanse, Forge, and should the blight take you, hope for a quick death."

Far to the east of Athra, where the great plains began to roll gently upward toward the Fae Forest, lay the Disputed Lands. Once, they had been the territory of another great city to rise from the ashes of the Aldunei Republic: the Free City of Freiz. Yet Freiz had long lain in ruins on the banks of Loch Awe, and those who had once sought its protection were bereft of proper defense and governance.

Brode and Silas had been tasked with visiting these remote settlements, judging the danger, and, if the people had to flee, determining the direction in which they should go. Given these lands were sparsely populated, they were rarely thought to be in true danger from a great swarm. As they flew east, Brode thought it an important posting – one to get him and his ill luck out of the way.

Unfortunately, things did not go well.

At their first stop, Brode and Silas encountered the deathly presence of the scourge not far away. Ghouls fell upon the town, and though quickly dispatched, it was a troubling sign. They sent some of the people north to take shelter in settlements closer to the Fae Forest in the hope of easing the area's attraction to wayward parts of the great swarm. But the same thing happened at the second village. At the third, the fighting was harder. By the time they reached the fourth, they were already too late – the scourge had come, leaving death and destruction behind.

Tendrils of a swarm could reach far, but this many ghouls and bugs wandering far beyond the control of the queen was something neither of them had encountered before.

One stroke of fortune was that the fifth town they visited actually had passable walls and a garrison, enough to support two Champions in bloodying the nose of the force that assailed it.

There had been ghouls in great numbers, risen corpses with their skin turned to chitin, running at inhuman speeds and inhuman single-mindedness. There were larger bugs in the attacking force, too, such as the great mantis-like flayers with their scythe arms and long legs and the hammer-headed juggernauts – great beetles turned nightmarishly wrong. Stingers descended from above, although thankfully not in sufficient numbers to pose any real danger to Erdra and Clesh. Luckily, giant skeletal abominations had not been present.

Fearing what might become of the Ascendants sent on similar missions, never mind the strike teams sent to engage the main swarm, Brode and Silas nevertheless pressed on. Yet three weeks of skirmishing and travel could make even dragon riders weary, and Brode began to feel the bite of their labors as they drew close to the southern border of the Fae Forest.

Thick smoke billowed in the distance.

Flying to investigate, they discovered a strange mesa of muddy red rock crisscrossed with maze-like canyons as though some force had eaten it from the inside out. Were that not peculiar enough, there also rose pillars of towering yellow, orange, and mud-red stone. The smoke issued from somewhere inside the hollowed mesa, rising to meet the cold gray sky.

They landed at the mesa's edge, and Erdra pressed her front feet hard into the ground, spreading her talons wide to listen to the earth.

"The blight echoes here," she said, spreading her thoughts out to Silas and Clesh as well. *"Though it is weak, as though a lone voice croaks its foul song."*

Clesh snapped at the air.

"There's no settlement here on our map," Brode said.

"That means little here," Silas said.

They took flight again, flying over the maze of canyons and weaving between the rock pillars until they discovered signs of habitation within the heart of the mesa: a shantytown of dark wood and red and yellow stone.

A cold wind whipped up to meet them, carrying with it the scent of burnt wood and charred flesh. They circled a few times before Erdra and Clesh found space to land on the outskirts of the settlement.

As the riders dismounted, a few brave souls came to gawk and point. Some fell to their knees and wept. The rest huddled around campfires and cook pots with their heads bent as though no force in the world could move them. Even when they noticed the arrival of dragon riders, they appeared neither elated nor afraid. They didn't react at all – a more chilling sight than finding a pile of corpses. All in all, there seemed to be too many people for such a remote place that was not even on the map.

"This reeks of evacuations gone wrong," Silas said.

Brode feared they'd played their part by sending people north.

Passing through narrow corridors of stone they came to what looked like a central location within the settlement: a thin, twisting spire of golden stone surrounded by the remains of broken carts, stalls, and spoiled goods. Something crunched underfoot, and

Brode discovered he had stepped on a chunk of hard chitin the color of an old bruise.

People continued pooling behind them, keeping their distance from the riders.

"Who leads here?" Silas asked. When no one answered, Silas asked again. This time, an old woman hobbled forth to meet them.

"Go away," she said.

Brode blinked in disbelief.

"What did you say?" Silas asked.

"We don't want more rider work here." She waved a hand toward the ruined marketplace as though Brode and Silas had done it.

This was hardly customary. In other towns, even in the Disputed Lands, they had been welcomed with open arms, then begged to stay longer as they departed.

Brode deferred the response to Silas as the senior, but Silas seemed too stunned to react further. Finally, he managed to say, "We're sorry for your loss." His tone was professional but not warm. "Not all of these people are from here, are they?"

"No," she said, throwing a dirty look toward one of the huddled groups apart from the main throng. "They came out of the forest saying some rider told 'em to go south. Brought the bugs with them, they did!"

Brode and Silas shared a look. So, the scourge had invaded at multiple points after all, and due to confusion or some overlap of orders with Oak Hall, small folk from the outer edges of the Fae Forest were being pressed south toward the heart of the problem. Whatever the case, it was a mess. Brode always appreciated when others could fess up to a blunder, and he imagined others did as well.

"Whoever told you to flee your homes was misguided," Brode said to the nearest group of foresters. "That shouldn't have happened. But we can help set things right—"

"Help?" the old woman squawked. "What you gonna do? Bring back me boy? His wife's dead too, and me granddaughter is sick."

In her fury, she stepped closer to the riders than most would dare, and Silas took the woman by the shoulders. Perhaps he'd meant it to be a comfort, but it had the opposite effect. She thrashed around but could not break free of a Champion's grip, and Silas searched for someone else to speak to.

"Who is in charge here?" he asked again.

Someone else stepped up this time, a young man barely past the cusp of manhood with a patchy red beard. "Goran was chief."

"Was?" Silas barked.

"Aye... he's dead now."

Silas huffed. "Who leads you now?" he asked, punching at each word as though the boy was slow.

Brode clasped Silas on the shoulder and spoke quietly into his ear. "Be gentle with them. They're most likely in shock."

Silas, like almost all riders, wasn't used to people talking back, obfuscating, or otherwise not being polite, orderly, and professional in his presence.

"It's not them I'm angry with," Silas said. He closed his eyes. A dragon's roar, deep and guttural, echoed through the winding rocks. The old woman, still in Silas's grip, looked afraid.

"Clesh is furious," Erdra told Brode.

"See if you can calm him," Brode said across their bond. *"I fear Silas is being affected by it."*

As if on cue, Silas's face turned clammy, and he drained of color. Before Brode could say anything, Silas let the old woman go, then shrugged Brode's hand from his shoulder.

"I need to see Clesh. Stay and find whoever is leading their fighters."

Brode nodded, then moved to guide the woman more gently back to the crowd.

"Words can't help, nor can they express your loss," Brode said. "I'm sorry some of our brothers and sisters made things worse for you. I promise we will do all we can to help you, but we need to meet with your soldiers. There must have been some to fend off this attack. Where are they now?"

She looked unsure, but the fight seemed to have drained from her. "Most of 'em died in the fighting. Those left are burning the bodies." She pointed a wrinkled finger toward the pillar of smoke. "My boy..."

Brode let her go with a heavy sigh. A lump formed in his throat, and yet bizarrely, perversely, he felt a twinge of jealousy for her dead son. His mother had cared – fiercely cared. Whoever the man was, at least he'd died fighting for a home and people who loved him.

His dragon bond grew hot and taut then, yanking him back from the abyss. He shook his head and gasped as though splashed by cold water.

"Such darkness does not suit you, my hermit."

A bond granted insight into a partner's feelings, often hazily but occasionally with blinding clarity.

"Forgive me," he said. *"A shadow fell across my mind."*

Brode unslung his traveling pack and dug out his rations for the old woman. "Give this to your granddaughter."

She took the food and scurried off without a word of thanks. Brode didn't mind, but he lamented that some folk didn't help themselves when it came to dealing with riders. He'd found that during a scourge crisis, people sometimes took their fear and frustrations out on riders as a sick patient might lash out against their physician. He wasn't wise enough to know why.

"How is Clesh?" he asked Erdra.

A rare growl of disquiet passed over their bond, and Brode sensed her unease.

"He snapped at me! So I've left him to bury his head in the earth... I've never seen him like this."

"Let me know if anything changes," Brode said, unsure quite what

to do other than push on with matters at hand. He cast around in search of the boy with the patchy beard and waved him over.

"Can you lead me to where they're burning bodies?"

More cowed than the woman, the boy gave a hasty half-bow and said, "Yes, Honored Rider. Right away, Honored Rider."

It did not take long. A band of ragged-looking warriors met Brode and his guide as they left the market area. Clesh's roar had alerted them to the presence of dragon riders in the area. Brode thought of them as warriors rather than soldiers, for there was no uniformity to them. Some carried spears, some swords, some plain cudgels, but a few looked confident with their bows. Some wore chainmail, others gambeson, but most wore no armor at all.

Only an old one-armed knight wore steel, which was scratched and dented. His beard remained thick, though both it and the hair on his head were white in stark contrast to his bloodshot eyes. He introduced himself as Kamen, having once served in the garrison of a border town in Athran territory. Many years ago, he had lost his arm defending that town from a scourge attack, and afterward, no longer being fit for purpose, the Master of Roles had shuffled some parchment and scratched out some words, and Kamen had been told to step aside.

"I lost my family the same day I lost my arm," Kamen explained. "So where else could I go but... nowhere." He cast a hand around the rocky dwellings. "Red Rock, we call it. A home to lost souls." He groaned from some pain or another and rolled his shoulders. "I'm afraid you've come too late, Honored Rider."

"Tell me what happened."

Kamen did. In recent weeks, people fleeing from the south had arrived seeking refuge. That had been manageable until people also started arriving north out of the Fae Forest and kept on coming. Before long, the gullies around Red Rock were teeming with rough sleepers. Supplies had been dwindling even before the scourge came screaming out of the woods.

"Seemed inevitable," Kamen said. "They came in the night.

Ghouls, mostly, but a few of the bigger bugs, too. Goran and I had formed a militia, and it was just as well we did."

"How many of you remain?"

"Of the two hundred fighters, maybe forty. A few of the wounded may yet recover. We've been burning the scourge and our own dead for days."

Brode took it all in. He drank in the wearied remnants of Kamen's militia, too. Few looked like they'd stand up to the next strong breeze, never mind another wave of scourge. One smooth-faced boy wearing a rusted half-helm was plainly still a child.

"How old are you, lad?" Brode asked.

"Thirteen," the boy said, and he spoke fiercely enough.

At thirteen, I was cleaning Silas's boots.

A pang of guilt rushed through him. As cruel as life had been at times, Brode reflected, it could always have been worse. His mother's voice seemed to ring in his ears and made him think about his good fortune.

Hot meals in my belly, and good new boots...

"You are brave men, all of you," he said, looking at the boy. "With luck, the worst is over."

6

MATTERS TO CHEW ON

Just as Brode was beginning to get the measure of Red Rock, word came that more refugees were emerging from the Fae Forest. One piece of good news was that a score of seasoned troops from a Coedhen logging camp had arrived with them. A dozen spears and eight archers. Sadly, the additional numbers would only increase the chances that scourge roaming in the southern forest would be drawn to the mesa.

By the time night fell, another wave of desperate people fleeing the forest had found their way into the passes of Red Rock. They became packed. Such was the chaos of the scourge.

Brode couldn't help but lament how fragile the orderly world was. Each person had their role in maintaining strong armies and keeping food on tables, yet in a matter of weeks, even days, the scourge could sweep it all aside.

Small wonder that anything or anyone out of the ordinary was suspect.

Brode also had Silas to worry about. Erdra had sent regular updates, but they were always the same. Silas and Clesh were deep in silent conversation, and while they showed no outward signs of distress, she could feel the turmoil in their spiritual presence.

Eventually, Silas and Clesh broke apart so Clesh could hunt for food. Erdra joined the hunt, and after assuring the people he would be back, Brode ventured to a canyon on the outskirts of Red Rock, where Silas awaited him.

With only the faintest starlight to see by, Brode couldn't scrutinize Silas's features closely, but he tried as best he could to interpret Silas's spirit. Brode had barely begun his journey to expand his soul and grow his spiritual power, but he had just enough in himself to take a passing glance into another rider's presence. Silas's soul seemed settled, although, for want of a better way to interpret it, he felt spiritually *bruised.*

"We should leave," Silas said.

"Leave? We can't do that. We might very well be partly responsible for this. Think of all the people we told to go north."

"We couldn't have known the fools from Oak Hall would bungle their own evacuations."

"Don't you think we ought to do something?"

"What can we do? Fly them all away? South is treacherous. North is treacherous. The west is the worst of all. East... east *might* serve if enough leave."

"Why are you hesitant?"

"Why are you questioning a superior?"

Brode took a step back. Something was wrong. Silas wasn't one to pull rank on him with such scorn, and even Silas seemed conscious of that, for he took a tentative half-step closer to Brode.

"I'm sorry."

"Something is on your mind. What was troubling Clesh?"

Silas averted his eyes. "That's between the two of us."

Brode thought that regrettable and reckoned Silas desperately wished to unburden himself, but a promise between rider and dragon was a serious thing. Even more serious than a summons.

They left matters there for the day and tried to get what sleep they could.

In the morning, Brode and Silas took their proposal to Kamen, his fighters, and all who gathered to listen. Silas made a compelling case to flee to the east. But they would not go.

"You need not all go," Silas urged. "Just enough so that the scourge loses interest in the area."

But Kamen waved the idea down and shook his head. "This is our home. For some, the only real home they've known."

"Many must leave their homes during an incursion," Silas said. "They do not wish it, but go they must."

"Must? On whose authority?"

"Athra's."

"Athra has no power here. What has Athra – or any of the cities – ever done for us?"

"Then go for the sake of your lives," Silas said.

"For our lives?" Kamen said, not angry, not even sad, just resigned. "Look around, Honored Rider. Our lives have been destroyed already. We've got sick and injured as well – are they to march for leagues?"

Some of the younger folks were more willing to go, but not enough to make a difference. Most had family who would remain, and they would not abandon them.

Nothing in Red Rock was as it ought to be. In the other settlements they had visited, the people had understood what was required and even had pre-arranged groups that would be ready to leave should a rising come. The people of Red Rock proved as unmoving as the surrounding stone, and those who had just emerged out of the forest were weary and feared entering open lands.

On the morning of their third day at Red Rock, Brode and Silas discussed their options over hard oatcakes and salted pork while their dragons lay dozing beside them.

"We could fly to Oak Hall," Brode suggested. "Someone ought to let them know what's happening. Then the Ascendants might be able to cull the scourge in the southern forest or else bring the forest folk back into the woods and send them north to Coedhen."

Silas pursed his lips, then shook his head. "That will take too long. We must return to Athra before the moon turns, as Lord Adaskar instructed. Even leaving now, we'd be cutting it very fine."

"Then we condemn them to die."

"We gave our best advice," Silas said, tearing himself another strip of pork. "If they won't go, we can't force them."

"Many of them will rise again to join the swarms."

"Maybe," Silas said gravely. He popped the pork into his mouth and chewed it slowly, with evident displeasure. Normally, riders could expect good hospitality wherever they went, being welcomed as guests in the nearest great estate and plied with the best food their host had to offer. Brode couldn't recall the last time they'd had to rely on their emergency rations. They weren't delicacies, but Brode didn't mind. He'd lived on such fare at times, and he took another bite of biscuit and pork without complaint.

As he ate, he said, "Leaving them to die seems wrong."

Still chewing, Silas frowned at him, and Brode realized his error. Chewing with his mouth full. A commoner's mistake. He chewed fast, swallowed, and hastened to add, "Sorry."

At last, Silas finished his smaller strip of meat, swallowed hard, cleared his throat, and said slowly, "Given what we face, a few hundred more ghouls won't matter. The fate of the world will not be decided here but at Athra, and we'll need every Champion there. Remember the first lesson."

You can't save them all.

No longer hungry, Brode set his food down. "Would you like more?"

Silas dropped his remaining pork back into the linen wrappings. "Not more of this, at any rate."

"As you will."

Brode started wrapping the food.

"Given what these folk are," Silas said, "I know this will feel especially hard for you. I'm not unsympathetic."

Brode dropped the linen bundle untied, and pork and oats spilled out. "I'd feel the same no matter who or what these people were – ah!" He gasped as a spurt of sharp pain shot through his chest.

No, not my chest, my soul…

That had been a new and unpleasant experience.

Erdra woke. Opening one eye, she peered fast from side to side. *"What's the matter? Are you hurt?"*

"Not hurt. I'm not sure what that was."

Silas gave him a knowing look. He must have sensed it. "Remember our lessons on spiritual development and how you must act and think true to yourself."

Brode remembered, and he might have said such lessons were far easier said and understood than enacted, but what he said was, "I remember, Master Brightbark. All the same, I find the first lesson to be… *unfair.*"

"It is the burden of our Order, Brode. You knew that before you took your vow. We cannot let the scourge win, no matter the cost."

"It's never won before. Not outright."

"No," Silas admitted, though he sounded grave again. "The thing is, the scourge only needs to win once."

Those words hung heavy between them.

He's right. What good will it do to save these people if Athra and then the whole world fall?

His soul twinged in pain again, and as Brode tried to comprehend what was causing it, Silas stood and strapped on his baldric. Clesh was awake now, growling low and stretching his wings.

"Fair morning, Clesh," Erdra said. *"Did you sleep well?"*

"My dreams were disturbed." The storm dragon offered nothing more.

"Time is running short," Silas said. "Clesh and I shall fly and scout for scourge movement. If Athra has become a great enough pull, we ought to see any scourge in the forest heading west, even this far out. If not, then perhaps knowledge of an impending attack will convince the people here to flee. Speak to them again, Brode. Make them understand."

THE OATH

The more Brode interacted with the poor souls of Red Rock, the more he discovered it to be a place of broken people. Those who had fled their hometowns for one reason or another. Some had broken their role, and some, like Kamen, had lost theirs and not been given a new one. A few had been called criminals for stealing bread to feed their families, and then there were the truly unfortunate, those people who had unwittingly contracted the blight and brought it inside their settlement, only to survive while others perished.

They had all brought or fallen into chaos.

Most were tragic stories and needn't have been this way. Among the Free Cities and the nations along the old Alduneian belt, the role masters were supposed to safeguard people from destitution, finding them new roles. If in doubt, the garrisons and militaries often swept up spare hands. Yet every so often, people slipped through the cracks. A role master might miscount. A role master might receive the wrong information. Sometimes, a role master simply did a poor job.

Brode tried to perform his own job as well as he could. He did as Silas asked and tried to convince the people to flee east, but by now, they weren't prepared even to listen. Most had made up their minds to stay or were too weary to contemplate the endeavor.

With little left to do until Silas returned, Brode withdrew to one of the red canyons outside the settlement to Cleanse and Forge. Of late, he'd been neglectful of his meditations, and given their current dangers, it would be vital to keep their supply of magic in top condition.

Erdra flew into the pass, then carefully navigated her way down between the looming pillars to join him. After greeting him and pressing her snout against his head, she curled up nearby to sleep, lifting a wing to cover her eyes.

Brode unstrapped his baldric, sat upon the dusty rock cross-legged, and laid his scabbard reverently before him. Its green, his armor, and Erdra's scales clashed harshly against the surrounding ruddy reds, ochres, and yellows.

As he began to meditate, he took a moment to feel and listen to his surroundings. The cold of the stone beneath him, the way the gully funneled the wind, the faint, sickly sweet echo of the scourge, and how the pillars created a forest of stone for miles around him.

Brode closed his eyes and began to Cleanse. Opening the connection of their soul-bond, he inspected Erdra's core. His human senses interpreted her core to appear to him like a sheer mountain, though one plagued by mists. Those mists were raw magical motes hanging in the orbit of the core. Many would be raw motes of earthen power, drawn toward the pull of her core, but others would be magical impurities, raw motes of other magic types Erdra could not absorb.

As her rider, it was one of Brode's essential duties to remove these toxins through Cleansing. Then he could Forge motes of her type into her core efficiently, growing it faster than a wild dragon could achieve naturally on their own. As riders only gained access to magic via a dragon bond, both human and dragon were made stronger from their partnership, but it had to be earned.

Cleansing was slow, unpleasant work. Carefully, Brode drew some of the obscuring mist across their soul-bond until it entered Brode's own soul space. A pressure grew as though a fist strained to break free of his ribs from the inside out. During his first lessons on Cleansing, it felt like he had been drowning, and even the slightest breath felt hard to take.

Yet the technique required deep, controlled breathing. He took a deep breath, held it for five seconds, then let it go with an extended sigh. His goal was to feel and hear for crackles in his breath. Crackles sounded due to his breath pushing against the magical impurities as he exhaled. By doing this repeatedly, the force of his breath would raise those impurities higher, separating them from the correct motes. Over and over, higher and higher, until it felt like a lump sat at the back of his throat. With a final huff, the knob of impurities was expelled from his body, and he could return the cleansed motes back to Erdra over their bond.

Time had a habit of slipping away while he Cleansed. Sometime later, a patter of light footsteps nearby penetrated his thoughts.

He opened his eyes. Erdra still slept, and twilight bathed the world in purple light. Having sat still, eyes shut and all focus on his breath for so long, Brode felt almost at peace.

He discovered a young girl approaching him. She looked to be all elbows and knees beneath her tattered skirts and woolen cloak, and she carried a mug and basket. Drawing up short of Brode, she curtsied.

"Kamen asked me to bring you food and water, Honored Rider."

Brode noted with interest how the girl referred to Kamen simply as Kamen. No title. No deference. When Brode had been a boy, he'd had to be respectful, especially to those in the military or those who served the military. Even Smiths and Fletchers had been above his Maid mother. Deference, role-names, titles, obedience – these things were order.

In Red Rock, such customs seemed excessive other than toward a rider, arguably the highest status one could be. Riders bowed only to each other.

"Thank you," Brode said, waving her forward. "I'll take the water gladly, but I don't need the food. We still have rations of our own. In any case, my body can go longer without food than yours."

She handed him the mug of water, and Brode took a swig. It had a heavy metallic taste and surprised him by fizzing upon his tongue. He wondered if it was fouled somehow, but after he swallowed, he had never felt more refreshed.

The girl stepped back and curtsied again. Such a small, mousy-looking girl, plain-featured and forgettable. When Brode left this place, he would forget her face, just as he had already forgotten the countless faces he and Silas had encountered on their journey here. It was partly a natural consequence of meeting so many people as a rider, but it also ran deeper, into the heart of the first lesson.

To know you can't save them all is to know you cannot care too much, else you will be consumed. Riders were trained to distance themselves from those they fought to protect. A perverse logic, but one that had served them well enough to prevent the scourge from prevailing. Sometimes, hard choices had to be made. Sometimes, people had to die for the world to live.

Brode took another sip of water, then asked, "What's your name, child?"

"Fiona, if it pleases you."

Out of habit, he followed up with, "Your full name?"

"I don't have a role-name."

Brode's sympathy welled. Having no 'role-name' was the polite way of saying 'bastard'.

Do I tell her I understand? Would she believe me?

Perhaps she took his silence for want of further explanation, for she added, "My father's name is Tanner, and my mother is a Potter, or they were – I dunno if they're still alive, sir. I do all sorts here at Red Rock, but Aunt Maggie – she's not my aunt, sir, but I call her that – she was teaching me how to weave, but our loom was damaged in the attacks."

Brode swirled another sip of the heavy, fizzy water, swallowed, and decided to depart from the first lesson just for once.

"My mother is a Maid, and my father is a senator in Athra. I have no role-name either."

Little Fiona did not look quite so afraid then. "Truly, sir?"

"Truly. Tell me, how did you come to Red Rock?"

"I ran away." There was a dream-like quality in her voice, as though she could not quite believe she had done it. "I was often sent to help the muckers on their rounds, and they would make me do most of their work for them. One day – I didn't plan to do it, it just sort of came over me - one day, we was outside the town walls, the muckers ordered me to work, then they took a nap and… and I just threw down my shovel and ran."

Brode could picture it well. *Her blood would have been running hot, her heart pounding. Probably half-mad from the fear and excitement of it all.* She had been lucky indeed to find her way to Red Rock.

"That was very brave of you."

Brave and foolish. What if some stray ghoul had taken you, or worse, infected you? They would have called you a true chaos bringer, then.

"Do you like it better here?"

Fiona nodded. "I do, Honored Rider. Goran told me that everyone has a place here, no matter what they were before. Kamen found me in the passes, sir. I'd fallen, but he picked me up."

She speaks of them both like the grandfathers she never had.

Erdra stirred then. Her wings burst open with sudden energy, causing Fiona to squeal and stumble backward.

"It's alright. She's just waking up."

Erdra yawned languidly, then settled and puffed green smoke through her nostrils.

"*Who is this young one?*" Erdra asked. Her words only reached Brode. She might have spoken to the girl if she wanted to, but dragons were picky about who they spoke to, even one as kind as Erdra.

"Her name is Fiona," Brode said aloud for the girl's benefit. "She had a childhood similar to mine."

Only I got to become a dragon rider while she had to run. Hot meals in my belly, and good new boots… Mother was right, I am a privileged bastard.

Fiona bowed so low to Erdra that she bent over double. "Might you be in need of anything, Honored Dragon?"

"*A roast hog with all my favorite herbs wouldn't go amiss, but you can tell the girl I am well content.*"

"Nothing is required, Fiona. Thank you again for the water."

Fiona half-turned, then hesitated.

"Speak freely, child."

"Sir, folk are saying the monsters will come again. Will you be here if they do?"

A blunt question. Brode did not know what to say. He dearly did not wish to lie, to make her a promise he could not keep, but nor did he want to crush her spirits.

Erdra growled soft and low to draw Fiona's attention. Erdra then touched her snout to a flat, round stone upon the ground. With a glow of magic, the stone shone diamond bright, turning pearl smooth and from red to leaf-green. There was nothing valuable or precious about it save the wonder of its transformation. Erdra nudged the stone forward for Fiona, and the girl picked it up. Erdra hummed, and Fiona smiled.

Nothing concrete had been said, no promises had been made, but the girl seemed encouraged all the same. Fiona curtsied again, and Erdra swept her tail playfully across the ground, then Fiona skipped back toward the town.

Once she was well out of earshot, Brode said, "Why did you do that?"

"*I was worried you'd tell her the truth.*"

As if to remind him of the need for truth, the dull pain in his soul pulsed again.

"I would have. Thank you for sparing me that. Still, we won't know for sure if there's danger until Silas and Clesh return."

"We both know that's wishful thinking."

He did. For such a remote place, there were simply too many people in Red Rock. Any scourge within five leagues would be drawn here.

Brode found himself considering the words of his vows again.

I pledge myself to the Order, which stands against chaos. I am the light that guides through the dark. I am the shelter in the storm. I am the first strike and the last shield. I shall take no love and rule no lands. Where others stray, I shall obey. No life will be beneath my aid. When death comes, I will make it wait.

The more Brode turned the words over, the more meaningless they became. How could he leave the people here undefended if 'no life was beneath his aid?'. In good faith, the words were to mean that they defended kings and paupers alike, that the riders answered to no one but their own. Yet, in reality, it always mattered whether the life in question was an *important* one. The poor fellows of Red Rock, the runaway girls, the maimed soldiers, the broken people – they had been forgotten.

"What should we do, Erdra?"

"I wish I had an answer, but on this, I am as unsure as you, my hermit."

Brode groaned. All he knew for sure was that he did not want to return to Athra if he could help it. He did not want to raise his shield there when no one had ever raised one for him. It was a selfish thought, but it was strong.

He thought about his mother. He realized now that a deep part of him had hoped to be able to defend her as well as himself. He also realized now that she had not treated him as a mother should. Yet as a child, she was all he'd had. A poor mother is better than none, but she, too, had rejected him now. However bad things had been, having Brode around made them worse. She did not want Brode's help, but the people of Red Rock did.

The people of Red Rock asked for what the rest of the world demanded.

"I want to help them, Erdra."

A deep rumble rose in her throat, settling into a low hum. Music entered Brode's mind. He knew it well. Erdra's dragon song, with all its soft melody and calming tempo. It sounded kind. It sounded like her.

"*When the day came,*" she said, "*to choose between staying with the Order and finding a rider or parting to join my wild kin, I had no doubts. Why would I wish to join other dragons who refused to fight for those weaker than themselves? My blood memories of all the flights are hazy to me, but what little I saw appeared as cowardice, fear, guilt, and despair.*"

She flexed her front talons, and her eyes hardened. Brode had rarely known her like this.

"*How could they not care? That's why I chose you, Brode. Even as a squire, you stood up for those weaker than yourself. Despite all you had been through, you did not shut out the world. You knew pain and wished to shield others from it where you could.*"

He thought he understood what troubled his soul. Silas had implied Brode's desire to defend Red Rock was fueled by his past, and if this were any normal settlement, Brode would have recognized there was nothing they could do. Brode had denied it, but Silas knew him too well.

Brode always found leaving folk to their fate hard, no matter who they were or where they were. But here, yes – his yearning was far stronger given who they were. All outcasts. Like him.

No life will be beneath my aid, he thought. *If something can be done, I must do it.*

The tension in his spirit eased, and his soul burned like a cozy fire in autumn. It had not quite been a full-blown spiritual insight, but it had been true enough that he knew he could not ignore it.

He could not leave.

Brode went to Erdra, and she lowered her head for him to stroke her snout and the side of her head.

"What if Silas does not understand?"

"He raised you up himself. He knows your worth."

"I hope for our sakes that you're right."

8

PARTING

Silas did not return until well into the following morning. Brode was in the middle of a Forging session – matching his heart rate to the beat of the dragon bond to hammer raw earthen motes into Erdra's core – when Clesh glided overhead.

"Join us on the northern outskirts," Clesh said.

When Clesh's presence left his mind, Brode sighed in relief. For all that he loved Silas, he had never been entirely comfortable around the storm dragon.

After telling Kamen where he was going, Brode and Erdra flew to meet Silas and Clesh. The land on the northern side of the hollowed mesa ran steeply down toward the edge of the Fae Forest. Silas and Clesh were on the open ground before the trees, Silas meditating, Clesh stalking restlessly. Green blood had dried in streaks across Silas's armor and the scales on Clesh's chest.

Silas opened his eyes, then rubbed at them. That was telling. Then, a firm presence passed over Brode's soul, inspecting it.

"I see you've achieved some insight," Silas said. "Well done. Please," he added with a gesture, "sit with me."

Brode joined him on the grass.

"The insight has done you good," Silas said. "You're more centered than you were."

"Thank you, Master Brightbark. How bad is it out there?"

"Worse than we feared. There's a small scourge chasm around a day's flight north. Bands of scourge are roaming south to the forest's borders. Clesh and I picked off those we could, but it's only a matter of time before the rest gather into a single swarm. If Red Rock had walls, a ballista or two, and a proper garrison, I would not worry... but they won't survive."

"Then let's strike each group before a swarm can gather," Erdra said.

"There are too many over too wide an area," Silas said. "We'd never hunt them all in time before they gather, and once that swarm forms, there's no guarantee we can face it alone. I won't sanction a suicide mission."

"So, we condemn Red Rock?"

Silas got to his feet and strapped his sword on. "We warned them. Their choices are not our fault." His expression softened. "We've left many behind before."

"Never quite like this. Never without some hope of defense."

"You can't win every fight."

Brode hesitated – he shouldn't bring it up - but for better or worse, he plowed ahead.

"If these were Athran senators, or Brenish Barons, or Risalian Dukes, would we still leave?"

Silas took a fraction too long to answer. "That isn't relevant to the situation at hand." He frowned. "But clearly, you have something to say."

"Were that the case, we would weigh the situation differently. And I don't think that's fair."

"Since when did we deal in fairness?"

Brode had noticed whenever small injustices were pointed out to certain riders – the Aldrich type – they could reason it away or claim that people misunderstood how, in fact, it benefited them.

Silas was not of this type, but perhaps his understanding would always be limited due to who he was and where he was from.

When Brode did not respond, Silas pressed on.

"These decisions are never easy, Brode. Never taken lightly. But we must go so we can defeat the scourge where it matters the most. That is the core of our oath."

Brode plucked up his courage, and Erdra lent him some of her sturdiness. "I find the oath to be flawed."

"I agree."

That caught Brode off guard. "You... agree?"

"In a way. More how we've chosen to interpret it. We vow to halt the blight and defeat the scourge, yet we hinder ourselves so that the task becomes almost impossible."

"What do you mean?"

Silas looked perplexed, as though it were obvious. "Well, for instance, why do we limit the number of riders to a relative few?"

Brode considered. "Only so many dragons wish to stay in the Order. Erdra and Clesh made that choice."

"Why not find the Wild Flights, then? Plead the case. Recruit more dragons."

"That would break the Pact," Clesh rumbled.

"Why should that matter if it led to victory?"

Clesh hissed and stamped. Even Erdra looked uneasy at this notion. For Brode's part, he had not quite gotten over the shock of hearing Silas and Clesh openly disagree.

"You see?" Silas said. "Even the dragons can't contemplate making the changes necessary to pursue the objective. And we're just as bad. Why should you have ever been denied the chance to prove your worth when you are clearly capable? I did not obey when I pushed for you to join us. My one and only successful rebellion. Trust me, Brode. I understand the urge to defend these people. I do. When we first arrived, that's all I thought about, but Clesh helped me to see reason. Athra cannot fall. Otherwise, that's the end."

"Are you ordering me to come with you?"

"No. I'm asking you…" He sighed. "Aren't you exhausted by it all? 'When death comes, I will make it wait,'" he recited. "'I shall halt the blight and defeat the scourge'. Defeat is the word. Not delay. Not hinder. Defeat." He looked Brode in the eye, and now his anger was plain. "How do you plan to do that if you're dead? How can we ever hope to finish this endless cycle unless we make some sacrifices? On and on it goes. Order. Chaos. Order, then chaos. We fight and bleed and die, and the scourge keep coming back. Something more must be done. Something different."

"And how is doing what Adaskar would demand of us— how is that doing something different?"

"We're only Champions," Silas said. "Come with us. Live. Grow stronger. Once we're both Lords, even Paragons, just think of what we could do to change things then."

"A fine dream. And all I must do is leave thousands here to die."

"What are a thousand lives, what are ten thousand lives, if one day we can destroy the scourge for good?"

Clesh nodded proudly at his rider's side.

"No life is beneath us," Brode said slowly. "That's also what we vowed."

Something happened then, something Brode had never witnessed before. Silas hung his head and ran his hands down his face.

"I knew this about you, little brother, but I had hoped I could convince you." Clesh snorted, and his eyes flashed with menace. Silas turned upon his dragon with a pained expression. "Don't call him that."

Erdra snarled, baring a single fang.

Brode could guess what Clesh must have said about him, but he pushed it to one side. It was Silas he cared about, Silas he could reason with. When he spoke, he managed to keep his voice steady.

"What is it that I don't understand, Silas?"

"Not to let your heart get the better of you." Silas shook his head. "But I should have known since your first ability manifested. What happened to you left too deep a scar."

Somewhere, the sound of twisting leather preceded a searing pain. Brode's left arm throbbed worse than ever, and he clenched his fist. Without consciously meaning it, his stone shield took shape. Once it fully materialized, Brode raised it.

"I'm grateful more than words can say for all you've done for me, Master Brightbark. But you're wrong if you think this is my weakness."

Silas stretched out his hand. "Come with me, Brode."

Erdra dug her feet into the ground. *"We're staying."*

Silas looked like he wanted to scream. His chest rose and fell heavily, then, with the utmost effort, he shook his head, just a sliver to either side. Then he turned and stalked back to Clesh. The granite gray dragon growled, and his voice rolled like thunder in Brode's mind.

"I always feared such spawn of chaos would cause him pain. Stay and die if you are too weak to do what must be done."

Brode did not have a chance to respond.

Erdra roared with savage fury, a bellow to shake the very pillars of Red Rock. She bounded forward, eyes locked onto Clesh, her power flaring. The earth cracked beneath every bound she took, and the ground shook so violently that Silas lost his balance and stumbled.

"Away with you then," she said. *"If we are so beneath you, be gone. And when we return, you better have defeated the enemy once and for all, else I will bind your wings in rock and keep you grounded from the sky for what you said. Go!"*

Clesh snorted and clawed once at the ground. Then, his breath of silver lightning lashed forth without a second thought. Erdra raised the earth to deflect his attack, then wind rushed in at such speeds that Brode nearly lost his own footing until he drew upon earthen power to weigh himself down. He called out for Erdra to back off. Silas shouted too, but his words were lost in the wind.

Yet, in this match, Brode and Silas were entirely forgotten.

The dragons leaped at each other, a bloody fight of tooth and talon. Clesh was bigger, but Erdra was tougher. The storm dragon unleashed his powers again, but lightning and wind were a poor match against rock and earth.

Brode forced his heavy feet to move, running for the fray and drawing his broad green blade. He had never thought he would use it to harm a dragon, let alone Clesh. Out of the corner of his eye, he saw Silas stretch a hand toward him. Brode raised his shield to deflect lightning, which never arrived. Instead, he slowed to a crawl before coming to a forced halt. A cage of silver lightning ensnared him, then pressed him down to his knees.

Grunting, Brode tried to summon more magic, but something about the cage must have affected his bond with Erdra, for her magic came as slow as treacle to him. Silas then drew his long, jagged blade and joined the fight.

"No!" Brode cried, but he could do nothing.

Silas ducked beneath the battling heads of the dragons, turned to Erdra, and swiped upward. She reeled back, her snout trailing blood. Howling, Brode sent what magic he could down the mote channels of his left arm along with spiritual power to will the stone skin to start forming. He dropped his shield, the stony plates snapped into place, then, clenching a stone fist, he started beating upon the lightning cage. The bars buckled, but Silas paid him no mind. He had rounded on his own dragon, slashing at the air before Clesh to keep the storm dragon at bay.

"Enough," Silas called. "Enough. I love you, Clesh, but you can be crueler than Master Vald at times."

Clesh snorted.

With a final slam of his stone fist, Brode broke free of the cage. He was on his feet in an instant, pushing the stone on his hand back out to form a shield.

"And you," Silas said to Brode. "You're a fool if you think one noble deed will make any difference against the scourge."

Erdra slinked to Brode's side and he placed a hand upon her warm chest.

"I'm not staying to kill scourge," Brode said. "I'm staying for them." He raised and pointed his sword toward the mesa.

"You let your heart lead you. So be it."

With that, Silas got onto Clesh's back, and they took off for the west, for Athra, for the Order.

Brode watched Silas shrink into the distance and managed to fight back the heat prickling under his eyes. After all, this was only the latest in the long list of rejections. His father had wanted nothing to do with him. His stepfather had made that painfully clear. To his own mother, he was nothing but a bad memory. For Silas, he had been a project – and a disappointing one at that.

He called me little brother, but a true brother would have stayed.

As Silas disappeared into ominous clouds, Brode wondered if he would ever see him again.

"I'm sorry, my hermit."

Erdra. He had Erdra.

Brode checked the cut Silas had given her. It was shallow, and Brode thought that had been deliberately done. He had not really tried to harm her. Already, the bleeding had stopped. He realized then that he still had his sword out and sheathed it, shoving the steel hard into the scabbard upon his back.

"I'm sorry, too. Let's head back. We have a fight to prepare for."

9

THE LAST STAND

Five days passed. Five days, one for each type of magic: fire, ice, storm, emerald, and mystic. There were five wild flights out in the world and five mighty Paragons who led the Order. Five days. Brode used each one to its fullest.

By day, he worked with Kamen to plan the defense of the northern passes. By night, he Cleansed Erdra's core until it shone, then switched to Forging. Kamen helped with this by sending valuable portions of bacon for Erdra to eat.

Altering one's heartbeat required immense focus, especially when the beat of the dragon bond could change its rhythm on a whim. Quick breaths sped up his heart, while long ones slowed it down. The idea was simple, but it was infuriating to master. Within these canyons and with the help of pork so many raw motes came to orbit Erdra's core that Forging them in was made far easier than usual.

Brode Forged throughout each night. He slept little.

Of Red Rock's original militia, only forty had pulled through the last attack. Three soldiers had recovered from minor wounds. A further thirty-one had arrived with the latest refugees from the forest, but seventy-four soldiers hardly formed an army. Some able-bodied men and women were prepared to volunteer, but there were scant weapons to arm them.

In the end, they managed to equip fifteen properly, bringing their fighting number to just shy of one hundred. The rest of the volunteers were used for other vital tasks: building barricades, gathering rocks to be dropped from great heights, preparing bandages, and readying pots of hot wine and water to aid the wounded. Lacking trained physicians, it was the best they could do.

Thankfully, within the winding gullies surrounding the town, there was a choke point they might try to hold. Within the choke point canyon were overhanging shelves of rock, which the defenders could take advantage of to rain punishment upon the swarm. Upon these, Erdra secured a waiting avalanche of rocks behind barriers of her magic.

All around was dry, hard earth, surrounded by good stone. If ever there was a place for him and Erdra to make a stand, this was it.

As the fifth day waned, Brode began to wonder if the scourge would even come. Perhaps the roaming bands had not gathered into a swarm after all. Perhaps Ascendants from Oak Hall had come in force to deal with the bugs. Perhaps he had caused a rift with Silas for nothing.

But then, as midnight approached, the scourge finally came.

Erdra spotted them as she patrolled the forest's borders. *"Warn the others."*

Brode and the watchers roused those sleeping, and everyone scrambled to take up positions. Their would-be soldiers stood shoulder to shoulder at the narrowest point in the pass, with a barricade filling the rest. Brode stood a short distance out in front of the line with Kamen by his side.

"I did not think you would stay."

"I felt it to be right." Brode faced the old knight. "Now it's time, do you regret staying?"

Kamen shrugged. "You get tired of running. I have regrets in my life, but this isn't one of them. What of you, rider?"

A difficult question. Brode thought of his mother, of Kuret Watcher, of his absent true father and his haughty half-brother. He lingered on his parting with Silas, yet while regrettable, he did not regret it. There was, however, that one matter...

"Just the one thing."

Kamen grunted in acknowledgment, but he didn't pry further.

Erdra reached out to him. *"Ethel?"* She voiced it as a question, but she already knew.

Many riders found their need for human intimacy diminished in the wake of bonding, but it rarely disappeared altogether. While technically breaking the oath, it wasn't unknown for riders to seek comfort in each other, though it was never public, never open, a private conspiracy in which the dragons had to play their part to cover their humans' indiscretions.

There had been times when Brode envisioned he and Ethel might be sent together on a far-flung mission. A few nights, far away from the overbearing gaze of the Lords and Paragons.

But a fantasy was where it had remained. He was marked as ill luck already. Were it not for the noble blood in his veins, he wouldn't have been given the chance to earn his blade and bond at all. And without becoming a rider, would Ethel Cawthorne of pure Feorlen lineage even have given him a second glance? Of course not. Brode treasured the chance he had been given, and he wouldn't give his detractors any reason to speak against him.

Yet now, here he was.

"Given the trouble we'll be in if we return, I might as well have broken more of the oath."

Erdra hummed wryly. *"That's as good a reason as any to fight your best tonight. There's always hope we will see the dawn. You may yet have time to bend more rules."*

Her amusement at the thought caused Brode to blush.

Then the first shrill shriek filled the canyon, heralding the approach of the swarm.

The blushing heat left Brode's face at once. He squatted and pressed his palm into the ground. The stones told him what was coming. Ghouls beyond count. The heavy pounding of three juggernauts, maybe four. Five swift-footed flayers. Thankfully, there were no abominations.

The stingers and carriers could not be determined so easily, but Erdra supplied what information she could about the airborne bugs.

"There are stingers. I can't be sure of their numbers, but there aren't any carriers."

That was good news. Carriers could fly over walls, land hard, crushing defenses and defenders alike, then unload ghouls from their backs. To face none was a small blessing. Without supporting siege equipment, the great wasp-like stingers would now be the most dangerous enemies tonight.

A final glimmer of hope was that this swarm was much too small to have a full queen. Without the guiding will and intelligence of a queen, this fight would be all head-on.

Quick and brutal.

Glancing behind him, Brode thought the stars seemed unusually bright, but ahead, as if following the swarm, dark clouds were closing in.

"Fires," Kamen called. Similar cries relayed the message, and braziers and torches flickered to life, as much a means to help the defenders see as one to weaken the scourge.

The sound of the swarm grew louder in the darkness, filling the pass and reverberating off the canyon walls and the many tall pillars of stone. Then, at last, the first ghouls came careering into the edge of sight, a mass of flailing, windmilling limbs.

The larger bugs – the flayers and the juggernauts – stood out like flag bearers amid the enemy ranks. Sprinting upon two upright legs, flayers were the most unnerving of the creatures, with razor-sharp scythe arms capable of cutting rows of men like stalks of wheat. The juggernauts' pounding weight caused the earth to shake. Half beetle, half monstrous bull, their strong hammerheads could batter down even gates if given the chance. If one managed to reach their meager barricades at full tilt, it would be over in an instant.

Brode stepped forward to ensure that wouldn't happen. A heavy smell of bile and death already filled the air.

I am the first strike and the last shield.

He drew upon the power of Erdra's mountain. Dense, core-forged motes of earth rushed into him, and he channeled them down to his legs.

No life will be beneath my aid.

The swarm came screaming on.

When death comes, I will make it wait.

Brode bellowed in turn, then leaped and landed hard, pushing his magic out from both feet. The dry earth began rippling in a radius around him, first five feet, then ten, twenty, more. He'd never created an Earthbind this large before. A fire raged in his chest. His bond became strained, and his battle cry sputtered into a gasp for air as he pushed to the edge. By the time he stopped channeling, his Earthbind stretched the entire width of the pass, and the ground turned to pools of thick, sludge-like mud.

A juggernaut got stuck fast in one such pool. It thrashed around, unable to extricate itself. Just behind it came a flayer. One of its legs sank deep into the mud even as its momentum carried the rest of its body forward. The snap of its leg reached Brode even over the cacophony of the ghouls.

Brode stepped back, already panting and aching from the effort. With a moment of respite, he checked on Erdra's core. He'd spent about a fifth of her power in one go; great chunks of the mountain seemed torn away, as if by the hand of a giant.

"That was more than we agreed," Erdra said in concern. As a

Champion, if Brode used more than three-quarters of her core, their bond would fray, leaving him vulnerable.

"But it worked!"

Despite it all, one flayer was already making progress across the bog. Its eyes were fixed upon him. Brode raised his left arm, forming his stone shield. It took shape moments before the flayer's scythe arm hit the stone, breaking the bladed chitin at a crooked angle. As the bug reeled and howled, Brode drew his blade and severed the flayer's arm in one fluid move, then he dropped low, slicing through its leg to send the creature writhing into the mud.

Stepping back, Brode took cover behind his shield.

Some arrows whistled past him. The best shots brought down ghouls; the unlucky ones glanced harmlessly off the juggernauts' armored hide.

As the first of the ghouls waded closer, Brode rushed to dispatch them, hacking them down as they fought through the sticky mud. No matter how many he felled, more crawled over the fallen. The swarm was like a tide, and he was but one rider. The ghoulish waters broke around him, rushing toward the thin line of Red Rock's defenders.

They would have to play their part, though Brode was determined to make it as small as possible.

As the clash sounded behind him, a great buzzing hammered above, and then the bulbous shapes of stingers descended lower into the canyon.

He could feel Erdra yearning to act.

"Hold it," he told her.

A wave of her irritation and worry crashed into him, but she held as the stingers dropped lower and lower until they were below their traps.

"Now!"

Erdra's roar was soon drowned out by the rocks and boulders set free to cascade down from on high. Several stingers were driven straight to the ground while the others scattered, leaving the rest of the swarm exposed to another aerial attack.

Erdra descended. Wings tucked tight, she seemed a flash of dark green. Just as it looked like she would crash, she opened her wings, veered up, and glided the length of the pass, spewing her green flames over the scourge. As an emerald dragon, the fire held no heat. Instead, her dragon's breath embodied the stone, pressing crushing destruction through the heart of the swarm.

Though great damage had been done, plenty of ghouls remained, and the surviving stingers quickly chased after her.

Brode returned his attention to the fight before him. He blocked clawing hands on his left, then gnashing teeth on his right. Needing to regain control, he funneled magic into his sword, drew upon his spiritual will, and cut a line across the muddy ground. A wall of stone erupted along the line, rising six feet high.

Brode turned, put his back against the wall, blocked to his left, cut a ghoul down on his right, and then drew another line across the earth to *will* a second wall into being. It rose to connect to the first, creating a defensive corner.

At his current rank and spiritual power, he could handle maintaining a maximum of three Eruption walls at a time, but he didn't want to risk a third right now. Erdra's core was draining fast. Stone chipped off the mountain with each heartbeat.

And now he'd turned around and faced the militia, he could see their line was in peril. In places, the men were already beginning to buckle.

Brode darted out from the safety of his walls to take a grounded stinger from behind. He cut through the weak point at its pinched waist, and the wet shine in its compound eyes turned utterly black.

He fought his way toward the line, rallying the wavering men back into position. Once done, he pivoted back around, braced behind his shield, and faced the swarm again. More and more ghouls were traversing the bog, and the surviving flayers and juggernauts were beginning to find their feet again.

Brode willed his two distant walls to disperse, then readied magic along his sword, intending to place new ones to aid their beleaguered line when thunder rolled across the battlefield.

Silas, he thought with glee, craning his neck to face the sky. But Clesh was nowhere to be seen. Rain fell in gray sheets. It struck Brode's face and landed in his open mouth. Under the downpour, he lost the stars, and as the world darkened, the scourge seemed to rally. The ghouls came on faster, and the juggernauts and flayers ripped free of his fading Earthbind.

Before Brode could place another, agony blazed over the dragon bond. He lost a moment to the white-hot flash of phantom claws ripping at his chest, coming around as two stingers crashed dead into the canyon. Erdra descended awkwardly behind them, trailing blood.

She wasn't going to make a smooth landing, nor one close to him.

Brode burst forward, abandoning his defensive nature to cut a bloody path through the scourge. The press became suffocating. A bone dirk was thrust into his side. His brigandine armor took the blow, but it felt like a kick in the ribs, and then a hand of ragged nails raked across his forehead. He tasted blood but pushed on, pulling on magic, fueling his body.

Erdra was all that mattered.

Suffering from a torn wing, she landed clumsily. Stingers pursuing her brought their barbed stings forward as they plunged for the kill. Brode leaped onto Erdra's back in time to block a sting with his shield, then split another with a desperate stroke of his sword.

"Back to the line," he urged. She did not need telling twice.

On her four feet, she bounded swift as a horse and with the power of a juggernaut, knocking ghouls aside as she went. Yet there wasn't much of a line left to return to. A flayer had cut a bloody hole through the militia and now ravaged the fighters at will. A second followed in behind it.

"They're dying," Erdra said, heading for the hole in the line. Charging into it, she lunged for the closest flayer and clamped her jaws around its leg, crunching through its exoskeleton. Brode blocked the creature's retaliatory swipe, then they killed it together.

The last of the flayers shrieked and threw the corpse of its victim aside. A torn arm spiraled off into the night, and steel rang as an armored body tumbled across the ground.

Brode jumped down from Erdra's back and rushed to aid the militia fleeing from the flayer. Blood and breath pounded between his ears, and his legs burned from the effort of running at such speed with his stone shield.

A juggernaut stumbled into his path with a spear stuck between the joints at its neck. Brode swerved around it, only just keeping his balance, then leaped again, placing himself between the flayer and its would-be victims. He caught its arm upon his shield, but the flayer's second arm slashed down on his right and struck. Its bladed arm screeched against the plates of his brigandine until its razor-like tip reached his hand.

Sharp, intense pain exploded up his arm. The flayer surged forward, knocking him over and his sword from his weakened grip.

On his back, Brode raised his shield. The flayer slashed at the stone. One strike, then two, then three until its arm was ruined. Shrieking, the flayer lowered its head, mandibles clacking to tear at him. The lashing rain made it hard to see, and the creature's foul breath turned his stomach.

Desperate, Brode dropped his shield and channeled his magic and will to form stone skin. He had no idea whether it had formed correctly – there was no time. Roaring in defiance, he caught one of the flayer's mandibles in his left fist, squeezed with all his might, then ripped the appendage free. The flayer reeled back, and Brode rose, throwing all his strength behind a punch to its head. His stone fist pulped it like a smashed melon.

Staggering, Brode picked up his sword. It hurt to hold it. His hand protested, and he felt warm blood on his palm, but he told himself he had more to give.

It was then he saw the body of the flayer's last kill. Kamen lay lifeless, his remaining arm torn from him.

Perhaps because of this, the wavering defenders started to break. Within moments, it became a full-blown rout.

Erdra's thoughts began to race. Brode glimpsed what she intended to do. And it panicked him.

"No, that could kill—"

A swooping stinger drew his attention, his shield, then his blade, but his stroke only grazed the beast, and it flew off.

"We're out of options," Erdra said.

"Wait—"

"There's no time. Get them out!"

Erdra came bounding closer to him, swiping ghouls aside with claws and tail. Brode assisted her and yelled his throat raw to call for a retreat, though no one needed encouragement. Despite their efforts, many of those fleeing were caught and killed, trampled, or bitten by ghouls to rise again if not burned.

Every small failure hurt. No matter how hard he fought, Brode could not save them all.

That was the first lesson, and riders re-learned it with every battle.

Once the defenders of Red Rock were either dead or gone, the remaining scourge seemed intent on killing Erdra. Brode focused now on her defense, keeping the ghouls at bay as she readied to work her magic.

She braced herself and pressed her feet hard into the ground. Fissures shot out through the earth from under her talons. For a few heartbeats, nothing happened.

Then it began.

A nearby pillar cracked, and then, with a long groan, it fell into the pass.

"Take cover," Erdra told him, her voice strained.

Brode ran to the edge of the canyon and drew a line along the cliff face running parallel to the ground. He placed two more to create supporting walls, then ducked under his shelter.

"Hold on," she cried.

Head bowed, eyes shut, all Brode heard were the cracks and deafening crashes as the world broke around him.

When it ended, Brode's conjured stone walls disappeared. Erdra's core was drained, the mountain reduced to rubble. His bond with her did not fray, he had not drawn enough for that, but the connection now hung by a raw thread.

"Brode?" Erdra sounded feeble.

"I'm coming," he told her, then staggered up, swaying as he moved and struggling to climb the mounds of debris and dead scourge.

The rain still poured, a heavy gray curtain, and the world spun silently. It felt as though he were deep underwater, struggling to breathe, to hear, to think.

Small wonder that he didn't see the stingers until they were directly overhead.

Then his hearing returned all at once in a sudden blow to the senses.

Hammering rain. Buzzing wings. Erdra in pain.

At last, he reached her. One stinger already lay dead, but a second drove its sting into her side.

Brode felt its cold tip as though it pierced his own flesh.

He wanted to scream, but he couldn't find the air.

Through some last effort, Erdra threw the stinger from her, ripping its abdomen from its sting. Black blood gushed from the stinger's wound, and it writhed in the air before falling dead to the ground.

Nothing else moved or shrieked or buzzed.

It seemed to be over.

"Erdra," Brode said, the fear palpable in his voice. He dropped his sword and went to her. "Erdra!"

Limbs shaking, she slumped down. The black sting still protruded from her side. Brode yanked it free. The wound wasn't deep enough to have nicked any organs. She could heal in time.

"Brode..." Her voice was a whisper.

He dropped down to hug and stroke her snout. "You're okay." He said it over and over.

"Brode... did we save them?"

He looked south down the pass toward the bend that led to Red Rock. No one was coming back up it yet, but no one was screaming for help either.

"I think so."

"Brode..."

She collapsed completely. Her weight brought him down, too, and he fell into a deep puddle. The water soaked through to chill his bones.

"It's in me... I can feel it."

The blight.

No. No. No, it couldn't be.

Brode scrambled, splashing through the muddy pool to check her injured side again. The rain had washed the blood away, but the scales around the wound were turning black. Even as he stared in horror, a few more followed.

One sting shouldn't have done it, not to a dragon as strong as her.

But she's weak, a small voice in his head told him. *She was already wounded, and she drained her entire core.*

"You'll be fine," he said shakily. "If you rest, then..."

He couldn't finish. If she was this injured, lacking the power of a core or other strong emeralds to assist, there would be only one outcome if the blight took hold.

Her chest rose and fell in a shallow, stuttering rhythm. *"It hurts."*

That broke his heart right there.

He cried out and thumped his fists on the ground. Mud and

blood splattered. *It should have been me*, he thought. He couldn't say it aloud. It would only hurt her more. He crawled back to her head, then lifted her snout and cradled her in his lap.

"Don't let me rise again."

He winced. He couldn't do it.

"We should have left," he said, his voice breaking on the last word. "Erdra..."

Brode gulped for air as his tears fell as hard as the rain.

"Please, my hermit."

Without conscious thought, Brode grasped on the ground for his dropped sword. He found it, his broad green blade crafted using Erdra's magic. A part of her was in it. He couldn't use it to kill her now – the only being in this world he could call his family.

Yet he must.

No one else was here.

It had to be him.

His fingers fumbled at the hilt, and he dropped the sword again.

Collapsing, sobbing, he lay against her, unable to move.

"I can't..."

I can't be alone again.

He reached for their ragged bond to hear her song, but the music faded in and out.

The dreadful truth became inescapable.

Though slipping away, Erdra began to hum. It was not her dragon song, but it soothed him all the same. With every piece of his soul, Brode wished he could take her place.

Across their bond, the rubble of Erdra's core reduced to sand, then melted away, leaving it bare. Then Brode heard her true dragon song return: bright, melodious, and as unwavering as she was kind, and brave, and good.

The rain still fell, but he could no longer hear it nor feel the droplets as they hit his skin.

His world became the song, became Erdra.

"Please, Brode."

He had never known greater bravery than in her plea. If she could be that brave, he owed it to her to find the necessary courage.

With her dragon song still in his mind, Brode picked up his blade and got to his feet. He stood above her chest and gripped the hilt firmly. His hands were strong and stable now.

"I'll see you again one day," he told her.

Then he did it.

A clean thrust down into her heart.

The dragon song cut off.

Brode went deaf again. Her side of the bond became a void. Its emptiness loomed for a moment like a night without moon or star, and then a wound opened in his soul as the bond tore away. Spirit bled from him as blood from a severed limb, only this was worse – far worse.

He thought he must be dying, too.

Then he lost the world.

He lost time.

When he came around, it might have been an eternity. Rain still crashed against the ground. The cold could not compete against the ice in his heart and soul. Erdra's parting had ripped a piece of him away with it.

His heart still beat, but he didn't feel alive.

When at last he moved, his muscles were sluggish and weak. He noticed that his blade still stood fast in Erdra's chest. When he looked at her face, her blank eyes stared back at him. That he could not stomach. Every instinct told him to flee – to run as he'd run from his mother's home.

But Erdra deserved better.

Somehow, he managed to close her eyes, then his legs turned to lead. So he stood there, swaying, cold and alone, until the rain abated and the morning sun crept through the clouds.

It should have been me, he thought. *What is a rider without a dragon?*

Erdra could have gone on to do good, to defend the living and defeat the scourge, if indeed it could ever be defeated. As just a human, he could do little. As a half-rider. Half a man now with half a life.

Eventually, a few people began to creep back into the pass. He noticed more of the fighting volunteers had survived than he'd first assumed. That, at least, was good. Dozens came, then more, until hundreds of people picked their way across the battlefield, crying over their own losses or else paying respects to those who had died for them.

People stared at him. He must look a mess, covered in gore with no life behind his eyes.

Little Fiona stepped out of the crowd.

"Honored Brode? Is it over?"

He managed to nod.

Fiona came a bit closer, then gasped and raised her hand to her mouth. "Your dragon, is she—"

But it seemed she could not bring herself to say it.

Somehow, Brode found the words. "She gave her life so you could have yours." The hand gripping his sword began to shake and bleed again. "It's the vow we both took."

Fiona remained quiet. She placed a hand inside her cloak and withdrew the leaf-green, pearl-smooth stone Erdra had created for her. Wordlessly, she handed it to him. With an effort, he took the stone, squeezed it in his palm, then handed it back.

"Erdra made it for you. Remember her by it."

"I will," she said, tucking the stone back into her cloak. "Thank you."

Then she knelt before him, and those closest in the crowd also bowed or took a knee. The effect rippled back through the survivors of Red Rock until everyone knelt and said their thanks.

Despite the outpouring of gratitude, Brode felt a desperate desire to be alone.

As he looked upon his dragon, the words of his oath tumbled inside him.

When death comes, I will make it wait.

This he had sworn. Well, death had come. They had made it wait. Red Rock would not be claimed, not this day.

One day, death would come again – for this place and for him. Brode did not fear it, for on that day, he would be with Erdra again. The only cruelty was that now it was Brode who would be forced to wait.

AFTERWORD

Well... that was intense!

Whether this was your first time reading *Last Stand* or whether you've returned to check out the updated edition, I hope you enjoyed the read! If you've come here straight after reading *Ascendant,* you're now well set up to move on to book 2 of the main series, *Unbound.*

Given that the original version was written in August 2020, I'm sure many of you are now reading it after getting to the end of the main series so far (book 3 at the time of writing). If you've come to the novella after finishing *Defiant,* I have a few thoughts I'd like to share below. If you haven't read the rest of the main series yet, I'd advise you to stop here, as there will be spoilers ahead.

hears the sound of many shuffling feet heading to Amazon or Audible to purchase the main series

Okay... I think they're gone!

For veterans of *Songs of Chaos,* you might be wondering why some elements of world-building were missing in the novella –

specifically in the magic system. Originally, spiritual power wasn't included, but now it is, yet the cycling techniques aren't mentioned here – what gives?

When I first wrote the novella, the idea of spiritual power hadn't yet been introduced into the main series. In fact, it wasn't properly brought in until *Defiant*. I always knew it would be an aspect of the ranking system, but each attempt to discuss it in *Ascendant* and *Unbound* felt VERY clunky and out of place. It seemed like too much information was being crammed in too early. In *Ascendant,* we were just getting underway, and in *Unbound,* there was already a lot going on with introducing the cycling techniques, elixirs, and jerky. Throwing spiritual power in on top of all that was just too much, considering it wasn't relevant to our main duo yet.

Also, if I'm honest, while I knew it would become important, I didn't have it fully fleshed out in my mind. Often, the finer details fall into place as I'm forced to write about them, and this was true for spiritual power as I battled with the first drafts of *Defiant*.

So, when I first wrote the novella, there was no mention of spirit. However, the stage at which we meet Brode in this story is exactly when he would be trying to develop his spirit. His stone skin would need spirit in order to 'will' the magic into something as sophisticated as stone armor in which you can still move. In this updated version, spirit is therefore mentioned – sprinkled in, but not dwelt on. Readers coming in directly from *Ascendant* should now get the gist and will then be primed for when it appears in *Defiant*.

What Brode doesn't use or even think about is the cycling tech-niques. I felt it would require too much explanation to use them, and a complete rehash would have been pointless for you. Just know that this was left out on purpose here. Clearly, there are moments in which Brode would have benefited from one cycling technique or another. For example, when creating his stone skin, Floating at the same time would have been greatly beneficial, given that it helps raise magical power to form a magical defense over the skin. When he creates the huge bind that spans the width of the canyon pass, he'd probably have Sunk his channels to pull magic across the bond quicker. While using his stone shield, he'd no doubt benefit from Grounding to help him deal with its weight.

A new element also cropped up organically in the polishing of this novella in relation to the summons. This is clearly a major part of the world-building, with every nation geared toward pulling their population to their capital to lure scourge swarms into decisive confrontations. As such, its influence would be more pervasive in these societies than it currently feels. The phrase 'As serious as a summons' came to me while working on this novella, and it's one of those things that ideally would have come to me while writing *Ascendant*. Alas, it did not. However, I like it. Should you see it pop up in book 4, this is why.

Finally, I'd like to talk about character. When I returned to this novella three years on, I was struck by how similar Brode's background and general arc are to another character from the series. I'm sure you know who I mean. While these two aren't exactly the same, it would appear my subconscious was interested in exploring this archetype. Thankfully, the characters have sufficient differences to make each one a unique exploration of a similar idea, charting very different courses through their lives.

I also had some thoughts about Silas and what happened to him after parting from Brode. In *Ascendant*, it is said that he became a legend at the Battle of Athra, earning the moniker of 'Silverstrike'. I can envision him there at the battle, full of grief in assuming he'd lost Brode. Yes, grief. He wanted Brode to come with him, desperately so. Even in *Ascendant*, when he's let Clesh lead him down a very dark path, he still wishes for Brode to spare himself. Yes... I can see Silas at that great battle, fueled by a need to make sure Brode's loss would not be in vain. When the scourge queen emerged, he struck first. He, only an Exalted Champion, managed to wound the queen, throwing everything he and Clesh had against her until the Lords and Paragons came to finish the job. His astounding courage may well have spared thousands of lives that day. No doubt he became a Lord afterward, though I'll leave what revelation he had in reaching that rank to the imagination. Later, in *Ascendant*, I reckon that killing Brode was the first push into the madness we see gripping him in the final fight. Clesh's death then sent him over the edge.

I feel sorry for Silas. Like many in the story, he came to see the futility of the never-ending cycle. He sought a way out, but whether it was Clesh's darker traits or being one lone voice unable to speak up, he first failed to conceive of a better way, then fell to the nihilistic solution proposed by Thrall. It's all such a tragedy, but then I think a world like this would be full of tragedy. A world stuck, unable to change because even small attempts at change risk utter ruin – and sometimes cause it.

Knowing what's at stake, how could anyone take such a risk? How might anything be done? Very little. That is, until one pot boy does something incredibly stupid...

Before signing off, I'd like to ask you to consider the usual things.

Please Review!

Firstly, if you haven't already done so, please consider leaving reviews for *Songs of Chaos* on Amazon, Audible, or Goodreads. It all helps immensely.

There will be a listing for *Last Stand* on Goodreads as well and eventually on Amazon etc. when the print edition goes live. Even though these are free novellas, please also consider reviewing both online where you can. It all helps in making the offer appealing to more readers who will then come join the community!

Recommend To Friends and Family!

If you've enjoyed the series so far, please recommend it to any friends or family who you think would enjoy it too. Word of mouth is still the best way books find new readers.

Pick up a copy in print

If you've grabbed *Last Stand* and *The Huntress* for free on my mailing list and would like to have a copy for your shelf, you can buy a paperback or hardback edition that contains both stories in one. You'll be able to find them online in all the usual places, including signed copies from The Broken Binding.

Please note: the physical edition may not be ready right away, Keep an eye out on my socials, mailing list etc, for all updates on it.

Follow Me

Discord: https://discord.gg/C7zEJXgFSc
Instagram: @michael_r_miller_author
Facebook: https://www.facebook.com/michaelrmillerauthor
Reddit: r/MichaelRMiller
Twitter: @MMDragons_Blade

Go and read The Huntress!

If you're now moving on to read *The Huntress*, I very much hope you enjoy this taste of my other trilogy, *The Dragon's Blade*!

THE HUNTRESS

For those coming to *The Huntress* via Songs of Chaos, welcome! To old hands who read *Dragon's Blade* back in the day – welcome back!

This story was originally written as a contribution to an indie anthology called *Lost Lore*. The theme of the collection was, well, exactly what it sounds like – stories or 'lore' that had been lost to the worlds they were set in. This was back in August 2017. That was a tumultuous period for me. I'd been in hospital that July, during which time I'd finished writing *The Last Guardian (The Dragon's Blade #3)*, then went back to work at Bloomsbury for a while before heading off to start Portal Books. During all of this, I was writing *The Huntress*. The stories for that anthology were supposed to be short, but mine came in at around 11,000 words. That isn't all that short... I'm not sure I'm capable of writing *short*. The scope of *The Huntress* certainly required far more than 11,000 words. Heck, add another POV and flesh out Elsie's full life, and you could easily make this a novel.

Perhaps that's what led to this rewrite in September 2023. After polishing the Brode novella, I thought I would polish up *The Huntress* as well – quick and clean. But six years later, I felt I could do better by Elsie's story, and I realized how this novella could justify itself in the context of the main trilogy. I'll talk a little about all of that in the Afterword.

So, from 11,000 words to 30,000 words. Elsie the huntress has had quite the makeover. I hope you enjoy her story.

For those not familiar with this series, it's worth noting that the dragons here aren't flying, fire-breathing lizards but fully human in form. Not dragonoid men, not half-dragons, just full-blown, vanilla-looking humans. They were once the aforementioned fire-breathing lizards but were transformed eons past for reasons you learn from the lore of the world in the main series. So, the dragons look like us, although they're faster and stronger. It's a bit like if a race of humans were all like Captain America.

One last thing to note. *The Huntress* was written after I completed the main series. Elsie's story was chosen because these events were hinted at in the books, so it seemed ripe ground for exploration. But in writing about canonical events, one issue is that character names are set. So we have both an Elsie and an Elsha in this story. Ordinarily, one wouldn't give characters within the same piece such similar names, but both of these women were named before I ever thought to write a novella that included them. And so here they are. For the avoidance of any doubt, Elsie is the titular huntress, and Elsha is a human healer. If you've read the main series, you might recognize her name as part of these historic events.

Okay, that's all for now. Enjoy, and I'll see you in the Afterword!

THE
ARGENT
TREE

RIVER AVVORN

RIVER DORAIN

TU

HINTE

VAL'TARRA

INVERDORN

BREVIA

LOCH MINIAN

CROWNLANDS

SPLINTERING

THE GOLDEN CRESCENT

TORRIDON

CAIRLAV MARSHES

COLD POINT

SOUTHERN

TH

THE BOREAC
MOUNTAINS

THE REALM OF
TENALP

1

THE TRIAL

The baying of the cusith chilled Elsie to her bones. She pulled back to crouch behind the thick trunk of the mangrove tree and pressed herself against it. Knobbly bark dug into her back even through her mud-red and green leathers. She closed her eyes and held a breath, waiting for the beast to howl a second time or else move on.

Wind whistled between the blades of towering sawgrass and blew ripples along the surface of the stagnant pools, scattering black clouds of midges. Elsie breathed easy. She opened her eyes. A silvery mist hung over the marsh, and save for the breeze, nothing moved.

Then, just as she began to think the cusith had moved on, it cried for a second time – a ghostly howl, cutting through flesh and bone. A second cry meant it had a scent for the hunt.

In her haste to move, her foot slipped on a patch of moss, sending her sliding down the twisting roots of the mangrove to land on the squelching earth. She cursed under her breath, then rose to one knee and twisted to face the direction of the howl. Better to fell the cusith before it could cry for a third time, but she failed to spot it between the tall grass and heavy reeds. The same foliage that kept her hidden favored the marsh hound more.

Elsie began preparing for the third howl by focusing on the grain of her bow, the wet, earthy smell of mud, and the way the tall grass seemed to sway. Her right hand ran through a ritual that helped to center her, touching first the quiver at her hip, then the feathers of the arrows, then the pouch on her belt that held her spare string.

Quiver, feathers, string.

Then the third howl washed over her like ice water, flooding her mind with sudden dread. She saw a baby lying rigid in its crib, his skin milk pale and his lips blue – but braced as she was, Elsie dispersed these visions. Still, the cusith's cry took its toll. Her body already felt spent, her limbs stiff and unyielding.

And now came the crucial moment.

After its most dangerous howl, the cusith – terror of the marshes – would move in upon its prey.

Come on, boy. Let's make this quick.

It was easier to think of the cusith as male. Once, Elsie had felled a female, not knowing it had a litter nearby. The creatures were no friends to the people of the marshes, but the memory of the whimpering pups still conjured a bitter taste.

She nocked an arrow, then drew it back to her cheek.

Heavy paws trod closer, and at last she caught sight of the beast moving like a shimmer among the reeds. The grass parted, and a large hound with shaggy green fur, a dark mane, and emerald eyes padded out from the mist. It would have blended into the land-scape completely, save for its white paws. This one's braided tail also had a white tip, the sign of an alpha.

Though alphas fetched a higher bounty, they were harder to take down, and after months away from the wilds, Elsie was rusty. Her shoulder burned from holding the drawn arrow, yet Elsie held her nerve, letting the cusith step toward her until she could pull off a clean shot.

The alpha's eyes met hers, and in their green depths, she saw the bestial desire to kill. A moment later, the hound bared its teeth and bounded forward. Elsie suffered a moment of hesitation. Her breath left her. She released the arrow, but it lodged into the cusith's mane, too high to be lethal.

Hitting the ground with a heavy thud, the cusith snarled, locked its mighty jaws around the protruding shaft, and ripped the arrow free.

On it came.

Elsie's hands shook from the lingering effect of the cusith's howl.

This was why you usually got one shot.

The beast leaped high, and Elsie dived into a roll under the hound. She felt the beast land as she scrambled to turn and take aim, blood pounding between her ears. She'd barely made it to her knees when the cusith pivoted for a second attack. It was so close now. And all her arrows save one had spilled from her quiver.

The alpha jumped.

Elsie nocked the last arrow, drew, and loosed without conscious thought. The arrow thudded into the hound's chest. The cusith yelped, then it crashed into her.

On her back, Elsie wheezed. Her coughing and spluttering were made worse by the cusith's choking odor of wet leaves, and her hands struggled to find purchase on its slimy fur. After managing to push it off, she made sure it was dead, then lay back panting with her eyes closed.

Should have kept my breath held on that first shot, she chided herself. A basic mistake. The sort of thing Captain Hogarth would have given her a clap around the ear for, but she forgave herself. A cusith alpha would be a challenge even for a huntress at her peak.

What else had gone wrong? Well, she'd slipped and fallen for one thing, even before the fight had started. That wasn't like her, but she blamed her boots. They'd been a perfect fit for years, but now one pinched too hard, and the other seemed likely to slip off. While odd, she supposed she could have been in a worse state.

And as the rush of blood and her breathing settled, she grinned.

It had been a little close for comfort, but she could still do the job after all.

2

THE MISSION

Elsie laid the white tail upon Marshal Balliol's desk. She stood back triumphantly and casually thumbed the top of her bow.

Balliol eyed the tail as though it were the hundredth alpha tail he'd received that morning. He was an imposing man, tall with a keg of a chest and thick forearms. In his prime, he would have been formidable, but there was a darkness under his eyes now and a softness hanging over his belt. Giving nothing away, Balliol finally appraised her by raising one bushy eyebrow.

Elsie scowled and held out her hand. "Pay up."

Balliol clicked his tongue. "Room and board and a sparin' of reputation not enough for you, lass?"

She gave him a cold stare. "You can pay me fairly for removing a threat from Lord Heath's outer lands. Do it," she added with a bite, "or I'll inform Captain Hogarth. And Roy."

"Master Roy is still your lord an' all," Balliol grumbled, though he began counting out silver coins from a fat pouch. He scratched a note of the bounty onto parchment, shoved the coins into Elsie's hand, then made a meal of busying himself with the cusith's tail.

From the weight of the silver, Elsie knew the payment was

correct without needing to count. She placed the coins into a pouch at her waist and then left Balliol be. His attitude hadn't been unexpected, but it still infuriated her. Balliol was too curmudgeonly and too vital to Lord Heath's administration to feel his position would be endangered should Elsie follow through with her threat. She wouldn't complain, of course. Doing so would only harden opinions, and changing minds was already as tough as chewing leather.

Leaving Balliol's office, she stepped out onto the streets of Torridon. Even at midday, the sun was obscured by a haze of muggy clouds, leaving the air close and sticky. Fishy scents from the town's many smokehouses lay over everything like a heavy blanket.

As Elsie walked, the coins jingled at her waist. The thought of picking up the order she'd placed with the seamstress before the hunt lifted her spirits, but first she paid a visit to the cobbler. Once there, she explained how her boots no longer seemed to fit even though they'd fitted perfectly before. The cobbler scratched his head and wondered aloud how that could be – he'd made them himself. Elsie assured him it was her feet that had changed since her pregnancy. Bewildered, the cobbler took her measurements, discovered her sizes had indeed changed, and let her know the price for a new pair. Elsie paid him, then took her leave, taking careful steps in her ill-fitting boots.

At the old seamstress' door, Elsie knocked, and an aged voice called for her to enter.

Wynda sat hunched in her rocking chair amid a sea of cloth and wool. A worn black mourning cowl obscured her wrinkled face, and she worked a pair of needles with a rhythmic clicking. Elsie had never seen her doing anything other than knitting. She half-suspected Wynda took her needles to the privy as well.

"Ah," Wynda said without looking up, "you made it back."

"That's right."

"Come to pick up your order, have you?"

"I have."

"I was surprised you asked for another one," Wynda said, nodding with sage insight. "Lord Heath ordered three swaddling suits, y'know."

"Of course he did," Elsie muttered.

Wynda cupped her ear. "What's that, dear?"

"Nothing. Did you make it or not?"

"Make it, dear? Course I made it, just as you asked. Nice pale blue with yellow thread. Costly, mind."

Elsie handed over the required silver, considerably reducing her earnings from the hunt.

"Thank you kindly," Wynda said. She bent to rummage in a wicker basket at her feet, then withdrew Elsie's order, a look of great pride in her gray eyes.

Elsie took it. The cloth felt soft as moss, so cozy and beautiful.

"He'll look lovely in it, dear."

"Thank you," Elsie said, feeling guilty for being curt with Wynda. "I'm sorry I snapped at you."

"That's alright, dear. You might be a dropped stitch, but one little hole doesn't completely ruin a tapestry."

Wynda clearly thought she was being generous, but Elsie pressed her lips together, feeling more confused than ever, and left before she retorted in a manner she'd regret.

Her tasks complete, Elsie tried to ignore the stares as she headed for the shore gate in the town's palisade walls. Beyond Torridon's smoky streets lay Loch Minian, and rising from it was the Great Crannog of the Heath family, built upon countless wooden beams. The crannog was connected to the shore by a long footbridge, which also acted as a dock for dozens of fishing ships and some larger longships tethered closer to the family home.

Seeing the crannog set her heart racing, and her mood improved so much that she could ignore the discomfort of her boots as she stepped along the gangway. A cleansing breeze off the loch helped to refresh her as well.

As she drew closer to the crannog, she was forced to weave between a throng of scurrying people loading the longships with heavy sacks and making them ready to sail. The sight twinged something at the back of her mind, something which wasn't right, but then she saw him, and all thought of longships left her.

Roy stood on the pier, chest heaving from hoisting thick rope, but as she caught his eye, he gave her a boyish grin. Other men enjoyed greater height, broader shoulders, sharper jaws, or hair not in the early stages of thinning, but none of them could match Roy's smile. None had an energy that made the dull world of the marshes brighter.

As she made her way to join him, his grin turned to mock bemusement, and he folded his arms as though studying her.

Elsie smirked. "Is something wrong, my lord?"

"Greetings to you, huntress, and thanks for asking. Nothing is wrong... unless you count my beloved abandoning me to chase a dirty swamp hound while I was forced to endure my family's dulcet talk of decorum and station and"—he yawned—"duty. Very dreary stuff."

"I'm sorry to hear that," Elsie said, stepping up to him. "Any idea when she'll return?"

"Not a clue. If you see a brunette kitted out in green leather and probably covered in bog slime, you'll let me know, won't you?"

Elsie laughed, then pulled off her mottled-green leather cap and let loose her knot of hair beneath.

Roy gave a mock gasp. "Elsie? My word, I didn't recognize you under such flawless camouflage."

"If only the cusith were so easily fooled."

Somehow, Roy's grin widened further, and then he pulled her close and kissed her.

A few of the men bustling around whistled or gave hearty grunts.

Elsie gently pushed him off. "Aren't we a bit close to the house?"

"They might as well get used to it. I've told Father that once I'm back from the war, we're getting married. End of discussion."

White-hot jubilation burst inside her. A moment later, icy dread plunged through her. The two forces collided, fought, and left her dizzy.

"No," she said, as though her insisting might make it untrue. And then, all in a rush, she carried on. "No, it's too quick – the dragons can't have built enough ships and broken through the alliance's fleet already? There wasn't even a hint of this before I left – they—"

Roy held her by the shoulders. "You're right. There hasn't been time for that. But it seems one legion sailed from Aurisha ahead of the rest and got the hop on the islanders. They landed in the Dales, and we can't let a legion of dragons run unchecked."

Why was he acting so calmly? How could he still be smiling? Sometimes he was a real idiot.

"But why must *you* go?"

For the first time, Roy looked anxious. "Because our King in Brevia has commanded it. All those with sword, armor, and horse. Father is too old, and it will be no good if a Heath doesn't arrive at the head of the Cairlav levies. And because I couldn't bear to stay behind while others fight in my name. It's just one legion," he added with a shrug, though he didn't meet her eye. "If we can't defeat three thousand dragons, what hope do we have against the rest?"

Elsie bit her lip. "I'll come with you."

"No!" His bright smile dimmed, and he sighed. "There's no place for hunters in the army."

"I'm sure an arrow through the neck will kill a dragon just fine."

"You're needed here. Aleck needs you."

"He needs you, too. We both do."

"Elsie, I can't stay. You know that."

This time, she averted her eyes from his and looked down. "I know... I know..."

He put a finger under her chin and tilted her head back up. "We'll smash this legion, teach the dragons a lesson in humility, the islanders will sink their bloated ships as they try to sail west, and I'll be home to fish the loch for harvest."

Elsie looked into those blue eyes she knew so well. To others, Roy might have seemed himself, but she could see the effort he made to force the joviality. She loved his good humor and nature, but sometimes she wished he would react as the situation demanded.

Before she could say anything, he kissed her, then pressed his forehead to hers so their noses touched. "Father needs you here, too."

Elsie snorted.

"He'll soften. You'll see," Roy said. "I love you."

"I love you too."

Two months passed.

Two messengers arrived.

The first declared how the King's noble army pursued the enemy across the rolling lands of the Southern Dales. All told, humanity's power numbered in the tens of thousands of spears and swords and heavy horse, enough to overwhelm this single legion of dragons.

Hopes were high.

Then the second messenger arrived.

He brought ill news of the battle in the Dales, including the names of the fallen.

Time dragged for Elsie after that, creaking by like a sleepless night. When Captain Hogarth summoned the marshland hunters to a meeting, she didn't go. She might have missed meals, too, were it not for Aleck, who still needed her milk. Holding him was her only shelter from the storm.

One night, she changed him out of the Heath family greens and buttoned him into the blue suit she'd bought from Wynda. His big, round eyes watched her curiously, and he rubbed his tiny hands all over this new, wondrous thing. A light giggle of laughter followed, sealing his approval. Despite herself, Elsie smiled back.

Later that same night, after Aleck had drifted off and moonlight streaked through the narrow window, she heard the door to her room scrape ajar. Lord Heath must have reckoned himself subtle, but she could smell the drink from here. He was crying, his breath coming in choked gulps. She watched his dark outline in the doorway from the corner of her eye. A honed hunting sense told her he was looking right at her, although whether out of pity, sympathy, or hatred, her training could not illuminate. At length, he slumped and crept back into the dark.

In the morning, it was with some trepidation that she answered Lord Heath's summons. Even more so when he asked her to join him in a small rowboat.

"It'll help to get away from everything," Heath said.

The skies were a more foreboding gray than usual as they lowered themselves into the rowboat. Not one to delegate every small task, Lord Heath took up the oars himself. Elsie sat huddled opposite, bleary-eyed and blinking fast to stave off her exhaustion.

Heath pulled at the oars in silence, his own eyes raw and blood-shot. Over the years, his hair had wasted away into a thin horse-shoe. She'd endlessly teased Roy that would be his fate.

Curses, but must everything remind her of him? How would she be able to stay in Torridon when every which way she turned, a dozen memories sprang up to taunt her, to mock her that they would never be again?

Despite the ominous sky, there wasn't a hint of wind out on the loch. The water lay flat, looking for all the world as if it were dead. As if the whole world around her were dead.

Heath rowed until the crannog looked no larger than a smoke hut, then he let go of the oars and let his shoulders sag.

"Had to get away."

Elsie nodded but had nothing more to add.

Heath cleared his throat. "You're one my best hunters, Elsie. I need you to know how much I value that."

Perhaps his phrasing had been clumsy, but Elsie didn't think so. He valued 'that' – her skills in the wild and with a bow. Not 'her' – not as a person.

"I'm flattered, Lord."

Heath gave no sign he'd heard her. "Humanity is in a dire position. This Prince Dronithir and his legion now face little opposition, and with the Dales in their hands, we're the closest region, and with the army shattered, all we have left by way of a fighting force right now are hunters."

Elsie tensed. It was clear where this was going.

"I've sent word to the Boreac family, urging them to send hunters down from the mountains. Same to the Esselmonts in the Crescent. If they can join the Cairlav hunters, we'll stand a better chance of delaying the dragons' march west until..."

But here, Heath ran out of steam.

Elsie darkly understood. Until what, exactly? What solution or hope was there?

"Do you think the King has a plan?" she asked.

Heath bit his lip. "I've heard nothing. Lord Boreac and I have exchanged ideas, given our predicament, but should the full might of the dragons land upon our shores, we'll be finished. As I see it, all we can hope for is much the same as before. The islanders still have a strong fleet, and the King has marshaled all vessels to join them. If they can sink enough of the dragons at sea, it might dissuade them from continuing. Then we must drive off Dronithir and his legion... somehow."

Elsie nodded along, but she didn't see much hope. "Hunters aren't soldiers."

"No, but you know the land and how to move unseen. The marsh offers better protection than the open Dales."

"Even so," Elsie said, "what can just the hunters hope to do?"

There were maybe over a hundred marshland hunters, a little more than that in the Boreac Mountains. Across the whole kingdom would be hundreds more, but even if every hunter and huntress came, how could they drive a legion of dragons back?

"Open battle is... out of the question," Heath said bitterly. "You must harry them, slow them, wear them down... if dragons can be worn down. Kill enough, and, with luck, they'll return to their ships and sail east."

Elsie stared past Heath to where the shoreline of the loch disappeared to the distant south, the blue outline of the Boreac Mountains rising far beyond. Things were dire, and she could not have expected preferential treatment, nor would she have wanted it. Not truly.

Without conscious thought, she heard herself ask, "Can I refuse?"

"I'm afraid not."

He threw up a hand to try to stop her from speaking, but she carried on.

"You'd tear me away from my child? Roy's child? Do you hate me so much?"

Heath winced. "Hate is a strong word. I've never approved... but you knew that. And your... *situation* will do my grandson no favors in Brevia – so I must impress upon you not to mention our *predicament* to anyone. With time, I can settle matters more favorably. Tell no one, or there will be consequences. Do you understand?"

If they were on solid ground, she would have risen defiantly, fists clenched and chest puffed. As it was, she settled for the fists, squeezing her knuckles white, but she did not raise them. She imagined taking Aleck and running, but he was Heath's rightful

grandson as well. She couldn't steal him away. Not after the family
had suffered such a loss already.

"This isn't personal," Heath added, a little curt. "Sending you
away. It's about survival."

Fists still clenched, Elsie searched to find the truth of it in his
eyes. She found it easier to read a beast's eyes, of course, but you
could see things in people there that they tried to bury deep. In
Heath's, she saw avoidance. He was keeping something from her.

"If I do this," she said. "I do it for my son. Not for you."

Heath's mouth twitched. He considered, grunted, and then
snatched up the oars.

"Captain Hogarth will be waiting for you."

Heath rowed them back to the crannog. Captain Hogarth was
indeed waiting for her, standing straight-backed upon the jetty.
Short for a man, his bow seemed large on him, but Elsie knew no
one who could blend into the landscape better.

Strangely, he carried a second bow over his shoulder, along with
several travel sacks. When Elsie and Lord Heath disembarked,
Hogarth approached, and Elsie finally grasped what it meant.

"Ready tae go?" the captain asked, passing over her bow and
packed supplies.

Elsie looked between her captain and her lord, fighting to find
the words.

"Right now?" Her words came out strained.

"Nae time tae spare," said Hogarth, though he at least had the
grace to look uncomfortable. "I'm sorry, lass. But you're the best
shot I've got. We'll need you."

First her cheek twitched, then her lip trembled.

"Might I at least say goodbye to my son?"

Heath nodded. "Of course," he said, as though he were being
charitable, and he indicated with a wave of his hand that Elsie
should look behind her.

Lady Heath, comely for her age, if a little severe, had emerged
from the crannog. She and Elsie shared little in common other

than the dark bags that had formed under Lady Heath's eyes and the rawness of over-rubbed skin.

Lady Heath carried Aleck in her arms, bundled in greens, although he still wore the blue suit Elsie had bought for him. Presently, he slept, so peacefully, so utterly unaware of the fraying emotions of the adults around him.

Elsie stepped as lightly as she would on a hunt, as though Lady Heath might scarper with her baby into the wilderness. Ever so gently, Elsie placed her hand on the layers of cloth behind Aleck's head, frightened to wake him if she touched him.

"We'll take good care of him," Lady Heath said.

That almost broke Elsie. Her right hand searched for her quiver, but it wasn't there, never mind the feathers and string.

As if sensing her pain, Aleck woke. Seconds passed by in which he peered blearily up, and then, knowing he wasn't being held by the right person, the crying started. Elsie reached for him, but Lady Heath pulled him back, rocking and hushing him, and before Elsie could say a word, a strong hand led her away.

"C'mon now," Hogarth said. "Eyes wide and ahead."

Out of self-preservation, she took his advice. She did not look back as she marched down the gangway back to shore. Only once they had passed out of earshot of Aleck's cries did she consider glancing back, but midway through the movement, she jerked her head forward again.

Eyes wide and ahead, she told herself. There would be only one way to return, one way to ensure her son had a future.

She shrugged Hogarth off but smiled at him, letting him know she didn't put the blame upon him.

"I'm with you, Captain. Let's hunt some dragons."

3

THE HUNT

Elsie had rarely strayed far from Torridon for long. The marshes lacked game, so she and her fellow hunters mainly guarded against the greater beasts whenever they prowled too close to settlements. Great wolves, the lean bog bears, black horned crabs, and, of course, the cusith. Never did the hunters chase the creatures into the darkest thickets, and rarely were they hunted in return.

Dragons were another matter.

After weeks far from home, Elsie stopped counting the days, and as weeks became months, each day became its own grinding campaign: a struggle for survival from dawn to dusk.

At first, the hunt had gone well. When the dragon vanguard reached the borders of the marsh, they stomped in with confidence. Many hadn't even worn their helmets.

They soon learned that was an error.

In short order, the bands of roaming dragons came with helmets on and shields raised. Along with their plate armor, it made them terribly hard to kill. The hunters had a supply of broad arrows, but these were intended to penetrate hide, not steel plate, and even if they'd had access to bodkins, their shorter hunting bows weren't capable of releasing with the power needed to pierce steel.

But the dragons shared some human vulnerabilities. They still had necks. Their armor still had joints, and their helms were still open for them to see – or for a lucky arrow to get in.

The war turned into ambushes, followed by flights into the reeds. A grinding game of attrition that the hunters knew they could not win, holding onto hope that the King might arrive with his regathered forces to help. Yet the months passed, and the only help to arrive were hunters from the Boreac Mountains and those from the Dales, where all leadership had broken down.

And though Elsie lost track of the days, she kept a perfect count of every dragon she slew. *Nineteen*, she reckoned as her latest target gargled a wet choke, then fell to the mud. Crouching low, she scuttled away before other dragons descended on the position.

Captain Hogarth sought to test a new tactic – pick a few dragons off, wait for others to crowd in to investigate, then spring a greater ambush. The dragons liked to head toward the fight, and Hogarth wished to accommodate them.

Moving back through the high grass, she was alerted to a deceptively deep pool she'd marked with a stick and a knot of string. She had to edge around the water, but despite the ground being good for the marsh, she somehow slipped, almost plunging in before just managing to right herself. It took a great deal of effort to keep quiet when such things happened, and she'd been slipping more than she'd have liked.

For years she'd been hunting in the marsh and never once fallen or lost her balance, not even while running. Since the pregnancy, it felt like the center of her weight had *shifted* somehow, and between that and her inexplicable new-sized feet, she'd been slipping and stumbling a tiresome amount.

Thankfully, she rejoined her spotter on a patch of dry ground without further incident. The young hunter from the Boreacs was covered in mud, but that was on purpose. White and gray leather might work well to blend into a cold mountain environment, but even the moles of the marshes could have spotted someone wearing them. The mud and grass rubbed over the white helped a little, but as dragons had far keener eyes than moles, the Boreac hunters tried not to get too close unless a fight was already underway. Hence the spotting.

Elsie's spotter gave her an inquiring look. She gave him a thumbs up, and the lad beamed.

"Might get my number to a round score before—"

The lad held a finger to his lips, and his eagle eyes darted from side to side. Elsie held her breath, then quietly turned to try to discover what he was worried about. She hadn't heard anything, but then her blood had still been pounding from the kill.

She saw them quickly enough. If the Boreac hunters in their white leathers were easy to track in the green landscape, then the dragons in their golden armor and plumed helmets might as well have sent up smoke flares. They were also big, all of them, each as broad-shouldered as the strongest of men. Elsie's childish notions of fearsome creatures with forked tongues and wings had been quickly dispersed, but they didn't need fire or talons to be terrifying. Why the King had thought to give battle against them head-on, she'd never understand.

It had been insanity. And Roy had died because of it.

Anger and frustration and grief reared inside her in turn, each vying for control. Her blood boiled. All thought and sight narrowed onto the closest dragon, some brute still arrogant enough to strut around without a helmet.

She drew an arrow and nocked it against the string, feeling the glide of the feathers along her fingers.

"Wait," her spotter whispered. "More are coming."

Elsie frowned, and then a few seconds later, more gold glinted some way behind her target.

Ears of a bat, this lad.

"Nice call," she whispered, then raised a closed fist, a sign to hold and be quiet. Whispering was all well and good, but you couldn't be too careful. It wasn't clear how sensitive dragon hearing was. Sometimes – even when the hunters made no sound at all – the dragons found them anyway.

Elsie's target, the helmetless dragon, remained in place, peering around and sniffing. One of his comrades joined him and asked, "Any hint of them?"

"Not a whiff."

Both had a growly quality to their voice, as though their true forms yearned to break free.

Scowling, the newcomer sniffed heartily at the air. "These bog devils get overconfident after a kill."

"Just need to find one, then the others come easier." The helmetless dragon huffed with displeasure. "This meek creeping is infuriating. Why can't we just hack through these swamps?"

His companion seized him by the shoulder. "It's not for us to question our prince's orders."

The helmetless dragon made a strange expression, like a strained form of chagrin. Elsie found it an odd sight. It was as though the dragon had never been distressed before.

"I meant nothing by it," he assured his comrade.

The defender of the Prince's honor opened his mouth to speak, but Elsie became distracted at that moment by a whistling through the reeds. It might have been a bird call, only it repeated exactly four times and then ceased.

It was the signal for the wider ambush to start.

Her spotter readied an arrow of his own, and she joined him. Already the sweat felt slick on her brow and neck, made doubly worse by the air being thick as porridge.

Unbidden, Roy's smile crept into her thoughts as though encouraging her from beyond the shackles of life. It set her heart to thumping as she honed her sights on the dragon who was too brazen to guard his smug face.

She wanted their blood.

Twenty, she thought as she took aim. His bright armor might have dazzled her in a land of sun and clear skies. But this was the Cairlav Marshes.

She was about to release when a howl rent the air.

Not a human cry, not even a dragon.

Elsie lowered her bow as a second howl swiftly followed, ripping through the grass. Caught off guard, she was unable to focus her mind before the third howl rang – before the fear came.

Ice ran up her spine like a frantic spider. Her hands froze in place, and her lungs seized with a sudden chill.

The dragons seemed unaffected, and now, as he sniffed the air, the helmetless dragon drew his sword. "They're close."

How can he know?

With her head bowed and shaking in terror, it wasn't long before the lead dragon spotted her. He thrust his sword toward her, crying, "There!" and a moment later, a javelin shot past her, missing Elsie by a hair's breadth. The hunter behind her made a wet gasp of surprise, then she heard his body fall with a soft splash.

Elsie still couldn't utter a sound, but internally, she screamed.

The lead dragon began advancing, cutting through the reeds with broad strokes of his sword. "What's wrong, bog devils? Come face us like warriors!"

Elsie's muscles finally began to thaw, starting with her extremities. Fingers tingling, she scrambled to get a grip on her bow and arrow again, even as the dragon marched closer with every second. He paused, looking down at her, perhaps curious as to why she was huddled in place and her movement sluggish. Then, like a wolf, he bounded forth—

And landed in the deceptively deep pool.

The dragon's battle cry changed quickly into panic as he thrashed in the water.

Waist-deep in the bog, his comrade rushed up to try and help him free.

Through great effort, Elsie managed to shake off the last icy drops of the cusith's third howl. She drew back the arrow, aimed, released. Its black tip ripped across the dragon's face, a red trail bursting forth, but Elsie turned and scrambled away without lingering.

All around her, whistling sounded in short three-beat bursts. All around her, bowstrings twanged and arrows sliced through the heavy air. Hard metallic pings mixed with pained growls.

Feeling she'd run enough, Elsie forced herself to turn back, crouch, nock, draw, and take aim. A flicker of gold moved between the reeds. She shot an arrow where the dragon's neck ought to be, but her target raised a shield with inhuman reflexes.

Elsie swore with a passion to make her mother's eyes pop. She loosed another arrow, then turned again and ran, hopping from dry patch to dry patch in the quagmire. Reeds and long grass parted ahead of her. Fearing dragons had managed to flank her, she tried to come to a halt but ended up skidding over the mushy earth, then tumbled sideways and hit her head against a mossy rock concealed by the mud.

Dazed, her vision flashing, she awaited the dragons, but it was a lone cusith creeping within the reeds, teeth bared and snarling.

Hunters were calling to each other now, interspersed with death cries and shrieks of agony. As she lay there, looking up at the gray sky, a dragon stomped into her vision. Smiling cruelly, he raised his sword – then an arrow lodged in his neck. Blood welled from his mouth, and he fell face down with a splash beside her.

Elsie rolled over so as not to look at the dragon. Somehow, she managed to push herself to her knees, only to find the glowing green eyes of the hound staring back at her. It shifted its gaze subtly from her to the dead dragon, then back to her. Its eyes widened to great emeralds, and then, quite bizarrely, the hound lowered its head, drooped its ears, and tore off, vanishing into the marsh.

Elsie gulped, retrieved her bow from the ground, then pushed herself upright.

The noises of the skirmish were moving off, so she followed them, desperate to find the others. Rising above the human voices, she heard Captain Hogarth's commanding tones.

"Spread out! Get around them!"

Pushing through wall after wall of grass, Elsie came upon two huntresses taking aim into a small clearing. They parted to let her slot in beside them, and she readied an arrow.

Within the clearing, ten dragons huddled around another, as if to shield him with their bodies. Their shields were peppered with arrows, and both dragons and humans lay strewn around them.

"My Prince," one dragon called, "you must leave!"

An arrow pinged off that dragon's armor.

Elsie held her breath to steady her shot. Though the dragons held their shields to cover their necks, she found the weak spot at the joint of one of their knees, then loosed. She hit her mark. Her target roared, and though he ripped the arrow from his leg, he buckled to one side, revealing the dragon at the center of the huddle.

The dragon's armor was golden like the others, but it also had ornate etchings and dragon-headed pauldrons, and he wore a crimson cloak that flowed from his shoulders. His face was hidden beneath a winged helmet, but with his unique armor and his fellow dragons so eager to defend him, his princely status would have been clear on its own.

Excitement gripped Elsie. If this really was their prince – Prince Dronithir – then killing him right now might end the war.

Out of sight, Captain Hogarth called out, "You're surrounded. Drop your weapons and strip your armor if you want to live."

Elsie couldn't believe her ears. Did he mean to take them prisoner? Even if that could be done – even if they could find a way to securely bind them – she did not see the use. The dragons had started this war for no good reason, and here they had this one perfect chance to exert a real toll on them. They should take it.

Elsie glanced at the huntresses on either side of her to gauge their thoughts, but they were both intent on keeping their arrows trained on the dragons in the clearing.

"I said, drop your weapons," Hogarth called.

Elsie took aim at the Prince.

The dragon she'd injured spat into the muddy water. "We will have no dealings with those touched by the Shadow!"

"Silence," the Prince admonished. His voice was more level, less growly than the others. More... human. "We've made peace even with the Black Dragons in the past, and the humans are not as corrupted as the Lord Guardian feared. In fact, I see little evidence of it at all."

He drove his sword into the soft earth, then removed his helmet and hung it on the upturned hilt. The Prince was clean-shaven, square-jawed, and might have been in his late twenties, although with their long lives, appearance was not enough to rely on. Raising his hands, Dronithir stepped out of his protective circle.

"My Prince, no," another dragon urged.

None of the other dragons showed signs of wishing to surrender.

Give me a reason, Elsie willed them.

"This is neither the day nor the cause to die for," the Prince said. "In the name of my father, Drakon the Fourth, wielder of the Dragon's Blade, I command you to lay down your arms."

With their helmets on, it was impossible to read the dragons, but their slight turns to each other, their silent communication, spoke volumes.

Elsie's heart began to race.

They aren't going to obey him.

A few did, though reluctantly. The rest did not.

"I should never need to issue a command twice."

The dragons shuffled together, forming a new band apart from their prince.

"The Shadow has taken hold of you, Highness."

"You do not know what you are saying."

"Come back, let us cut our way free."

The Prince's expression flickered through despair before settling on determination. He turned his back on his dragons.

"Who leads you, humans? Step forth."

After a tense wait, Captain Hogarth strode out of his cover and into the clearing, holding his bow by his side. Slight of frame, weather-worn, and bearded, Hogarth cut a perfect opposite to the Prince.

Elsie's fear overcame her training. "Captain, no!"

"Quiet," Hogarth called, and Elsie bit back further words. Her comrades on either side gave her dark, sidelong glances, and rightly so, for at least one of the dragons was now looking directly toward them.

Hogarth carefully carried on, and Dronithir ushered him closer.

"Have the dark gods ever whispered to you, human?" the Prince asked.

"We hav'nae a clue what yer talking about," said the captain. "We were just living our lives before, far from you. We just want things to return to that."

"I believe you," said the Prince. He turned to address his dragons. "I sense no otherworldly power from them. I do not see the void of dark powers within their eyes. Human, why do you wear clothes in such colors?"

"Tae trick your eyes, dragon."

"Quite," Dronithir said. "They evade through cloth and skill, not by the aid of shadow and darkness. This is not the war we should be fighting."

He spoke with such conviction that the huntress to Elsie's right lowered her bow, but Elsie kept hers securely in place. She didn't believe a word of it. This reeked of playing for time. They should have taken the dragons down, then vanished into the marsh like cusith.

Dronithir seemed to convince three more dragons to his way of thinking, yet even as they lowered their swords, fresh whistling rang from the east. Two quick blasts, followed by a third rising note, which was then repeated.

A warning.

Enemies were coming.

Dronithir frowned, pulled Hogarth close, and spoke low to him.

Damn it, Elsie thought as she shifted to adjust her position and aim. Prince Dronithir had blundered into saving himself by shifting Hogarth toward him, blocking her line of sight.

The whistling ended, then bows clapped, steel rang, running feet splashed through shallow pools, and six more dragons burst into the clearing, two with blood running from their blades.

"Secure the Prince!"

Perhaps this dragon warrior was deluded, thinking that Hogarth somehow had the Prince pinned or threatened. Perhaps the warrior's blood was too hot to see the reality for what it was. Or perhaps it was as Elsie suspected, and this parley had been a ruse. Elsie did not know, and could not know, but when that warrior severed Hogarth's leg beneath the knee, she had only one response.

As her captain fell screaming, dark blood spurting from his wound, she cried, "Loose! Loose!"

A dozen bowstrings thrummed. Her own arrow caught the hot-headed warrior at his armpit, and she drew another, trying to find the Prince within the sudden chaos.

The first barrage took two dragons down, and the second took down three. Then the remaining dragons leaped out of the clearing into the thicket of reeds and grass.

The huntress to Elsie's left was caught and killed in an eye blink. Elsie pivoted, dropped, and loosed an arrow aiming up. The arrow struck the dragon's helmet with a clang, and he wobbled, momentarily dazed, before a second shot followed from nearby. Two blows to the head from this close would do the trick. Strong as they were, dragons still had skulls of bone and soft brains inside, and this dragon fell backward.

A scream from behind.

Elsie turned to find her comrade being yanked bodily through the reeds. Unable to get a clear shot at the assailant, Elsie leaped after her. Entering the clearing, she found the dragon struggling to move, an arrow through the weaker plates at the back of his leg, though he still had the strength to drag the huntress through the mud while she kicked and struggled in vain.

Elsie loosed an arrow only meters away. The arrow struck with such ferocity as to leave a burn ring where it hit the gold plate. The dragon growled but didn't slow down, and one savage blow with his fist was enough to snap his prey's neck.

Elsie hit him again, then, stepping back, she drew and loosed a third arrow, moving so fast she stumbled and fell. None of her arrows had drawn blood, but whether from the blunt force of her strikes or something else, the dragon slumped face down and lay still.

And as sudden as the chaos had started, all went quiet. Not even a groan of pain. No bird calls, real or faked. No stir of the wind through the weeds. Then again, Elsie couldn't hear much over her own heaving breaths.

Scrambling back to her feet, she searched for Captain Hogarth. He lay face up, maimed and bleeding, and while his eyes were still open, he mouthed silently as though lost in a trance. Elsie stumbled through the shallow water to his side before falling to her knees again, her hands shaking, lost as to what to do.

She was a huntress, not a healer.

It was then she saw the dragon prince lying nearby. An arrow protruded from his waist; blood seeped from a wound to his head, and his eyes were closed. Elsie tried to draw an arrow, only to discover the string had snapped free from the bottom limb of her bow. No matter. She dropped the bow, unsheathed her thick hunting knife instead, and crept toward the Prince. Under his armor, she couldn't tell if his chest still rose and fell, but she'd make sure he was dead. Let this Dragon King in the east taste the same bitterness she had.

Within reach of his neck, Elsie struck.

The Prince opened his eyes, and with a roar he caught her arm, squeezing so hard she lost her grip on her knife. Then, rising with sudden strength, he threw her off. Elsie spun, then tumbled head over heels before crashing through water and mud. Pain exploded from her shoulder and chest, and the world seemed to turn to shadow, to light, to shadow again.

I'm dying, she thought as the darkness pressed in.

Aleck flickered through her mind, and his babbles of joy and his tiny hand gripping her finger anchored her back to the light. She could not, would not die. Not now. Not here.

I have to go home.

As Elsie battled the darkness, other voices entered the clearing. They sounded fuzzy, as though vibrating through water. Something about survivors and wounded.

A pair of hands gripped her and turned her over. Elsie's eyes stung under the cold sky, and through flashing vision, she saw a woman she did not know kneeling over her. The woman called out something, but Elsie couldn't make sense of it, for the woman's long blonde braid was swaying above her face, and watching its entrancing rhythm, Elsie finally succumbed to the dark.

4

THE HEALER

Elsie hurtled through the reeds, which parted before her like water. She didn't question it. Roy was calling her. He was in danger. He needed her.

On all sides, the dragons roared, trying to find her, but no matter how fast she ran, Roy's voice sounded far away. The reeds grew taller until they loomed on all sides like willowy mountains, bending, leaning over, suffocating her.

Elsie dropped to her hands and knees and crawled. Roy was still calling, and now Aleck, too, was out there – they both needed her. The reeds coiled around her, lifting her up, and she thrashed and kicked and yelled, reaching for her knife, but it wasn't there—

Elsie woke to a chill darkness. Breathing hard, she blinked, and a hazy ball of candlelight flitted closer toward her. As her vision sharpened, she discovered the candle bearer was a Boreac huntress in white and gray leathers. Even in the weak glow, she recognized the long braid of blonde hair. She'd been the one who'd knelt over Elsie in the marsh. She seemed so young.

"Welcome back, Elsie," the girl said. She felt at Elise's forehead, then held her wrist between thumb and forefinger. "Are you in pain?"

Elsie couldn't be sure. She didn't feel much, so she tried to move—

"Ah," she winced, inhaling sharply through clenched teeth. Her left hand moved instinctually to hold the right side of her chest, which stabbed with pain.

The huntress lifted Elsie's hand and moved it back to her side. "You broke a couple of ribs, and your right shoulder was dislocated. I set it back in place, but if you want to regain full use of your arm, you'd better keep it still for a while."

Elsie only noticed then that her right arm was immobilized in a sling. Currently, she lacked the energy to move it, even if she wanted to. This girl might wear the leathers of a huntress, but she was clearly a healer.

"You have me at a disadvantage," Elsie said. Her throat felt dry as sand. "I'd like to thank you properly."

"I'm Elsha."

"Thank you, Elsha."

"Just doing my part." She let go of Elsie's wrist. "Pulse is normal. Well, as normal as we might expect."

As Elsha checked on the sling, Elsie asked her, "Why are you wearing hunter leathers?"

"Seemed the natural thing to wear after Lord Boreac reassigned many of us from the army."

"You were with the army?"

"For all the good we did," Elsha said. "These dragons can tear us apart. I've never seen so many wounded... many of them I couldn't help at all."

Elsie wondered, horribly, whether Roy had been among those men she'd seen savaged beyond recognition.

"It's not been a fair fight," Elsie said.

Elsha pulled back from inspecting the sling, seemingly satisfied.

"Not really, no. Especially as these dragons also seem to heal quickly."

That caught Elsie off guard. Her heart pounded, and the stabbing in her chest pierced deeper. Taking shallow breaths, she said, "What do you mean? How do you know that?"

"I've treated some," Elsha said as though it were perfectly obvious. "Even their deep wounds knit back twice as fast as a human's, sometimes without scars. Their bones mend quicker, too."

Anger boiled in Elsie, though it took her sluggish mind a moment to catch up as to why.

"Why would you help them?"

"Because I'm a healer."

Elsie's sluggish mind now started racing. There had been a lot of bodies in that clearing in the marsh, and not all of them had been dead. One – there was one she'd not been able to finish.

"Did their prince live?"

Elsha looked confused for the first time.

"Their prince!" In her urgency, she tried to sit upright, but her right side protested with dizzying pain.

Elsha pressed her back down. "I said don't move. I'll strap you down if I have to."

Spluttering, Elsie rolled her head onto her shoulder, trying to hide from the healer's admonishing stare.

Her next breath caught in her throat. It couldn't be, not... not lying in the very bed beside her. With just the haze of a lone candle to see by, it was hard to tell for sure if it was the Prince, but whoever he was, the patient was secured to the bedframe by leather straps and steel manacles.

"Who's that?" she asked weakly.

"One of the dragons, if you must know," Elsha said, her bedside manner slipping. "He's out cold like you were, and not even they can break free of all those restraints. Please, Elsie, just rest. That's all you need to do right now."

As though he were listening in and wished to communicate, the dragon began groaning in his sleep. Elsha hurried to check on him. As her candlelight brought her patient into full relief, Elsie's insides clenched. His face was partially obscured by bloody bandages, but without a doubt, it was the Prince.

When Elsie came around again, her head spun. The last thing she remembered was discovering Prince Dronithir in the bed beside her, and there he remained, bound and trussed like the animal he was. She'd fallen asleep with her neck twisted awkwardly, and a knotted cramp had gathered there. She righted herself, grunted against the pain in her chest, shoulder, and now neck, then discovered it was morning.

A pale dawn and a current of cool air rushed in through an open window. While welcome, the breeze could not quite dispel the musty, unwashed scent of the infirmary nor the pungent odor of garlic from bowls of poultices.

Elsie also discovered another Boreac huntress sitting at the end of her bed. It wasn't Elsha, the healer, but Captain Luna, leader of the Boreac hunters. Even seated, there was something unnerving in her bearing, in the foreboding manner in which she sat so still. Luna's short black hair and narrow black eyes gave her the look of a prowling mountain lynx.

"You're awake," Luna said. "How are you feeling?"

"Painfu—"

"Well, to be expected," Luna barreled on. "I'm afraid Captain Hogarth is in a critical condition, leaving you as his most senior Cairlav hunter. However, as you yourself are incapacitated, I'll need a nominee to fulfill your duties until you recover."

Elsie processed this rush of information slowly.

"I can't be the most senior Cairlav hunter left. What about Malcolm?"

"He and his patrol are currently missing."

Elsie set her jaw. Missing was as good as dead these days.

"Alright. Then I name Dunsten. He knows the eastern marsh as well as any."

Captain Luna rose. "You'll be kept appraised of your captain's condition. Otherwise, rest up."

With that, Luna left.

Elsie tried to sit upright again, but her injury told her that wasn't happening. So she lay there, listening to the healers as they bustled from wounded to wounded.

As far as she could tell, there were a dozen other patients in this hut, with the dragon prince to her left and a fellow hunter to her right. The hunter seemed to be in a deep sleep, though the healers weren't concerned. Anyone else she might speak to was too far away, so she was content to keep to herself and listen in on everything she could.

And from what she overheard, she understood they were in Farlen, a settlement in the Boreac Mountains. That helped explain why there was a chill breeze. Elsha returned twice, though she was unwilling to humor Elsie further on the topic of the dragons. Elsie also thought she lingered too long at the Prince's side, longer than with the other wounded. Changing bandages didn't take *that* long.

And then it was night again, and the chattering and groans of the wounded fell quiet.

All were asleep, save for Elsie.

She lay there, staring up into the dark recesses of the timber beams, unable to drift off, unable to settle her rattling thoughts. She wished to sleep, but she didn't wish to dream of Aleck or Roy either.

And the damned prince of dragons was lying right beside her, as if mocking her. Without her bow or knife, there was nothing she could do. Could dragons even be strangled with only a human's strength?

Driven by an unknown force, she pushed through the pain and sat upright. Alone in the dark, her heavy breaths sounded like drumbeats. Cold silver light entered the hut from shutters left partially open, and something in its path glinted upon a table. Scissors.

The pain in Elsie's chest ebbed away as she leaned forward to get a better view. The reflected light from the scissors was dull, meaning they were probably simple iron, left out where a healer had been cutting rolls of bandages.

Leaning on her good side, Elsie managed to step out of her bed. It wasn't easy. Her feet felt unstable, and her legs worked against her, but through sheer stubbornness, she approached the table. On her way, she knocked her bedpan over. Thankfully, it was empty, but the ceramic bowl rattled shrilly in the darkness. A few steps more, and she reached the table and grabbed the scissors.

"What's that?" someone in the darkness asked groggily.

Elsie turned, eyes fixed on her prey.

Someone called, but she didn't hear them. Everything narrowed in on the Prince and the bloody bandages covering his face.

She shuffled toward him with the scissors raised. Mere feet away, he woke up. The bandages around his head covered one eye, but the other met her own. He didn't yell. He didn't try to rip free of his restraints. He didn't try anything.

Something banged behind her as Elsie reached the Prince's bedside. She clenched her fist tighter around the scissors' handle, the blades pointed down, and drove her fist toward his stomach—

But a pair of strong hands caught her forearm. The tips of the scissors cut through the sheets and drew forth a spurt of red, but the cut wasn't deep.

Then more hands seized her from behind and dragged her away.

"No," she said, afraid of how hoarse she sounded. "No..."

She wanted to resist but couldn't. She crumpled, the pain in her chest now a fire that grew hotter with every breath. Tears wet her face. Mingled voices blurred into so much whistling wind, and Elsie fell into darkness again.

This time, when she woke, she could feel the bonds at her one good wrist, her legs, and her feet. She strained against them but barely had the energy left to weep. It was all she could do to keep her wits, remember where she was and who she was, but failure pierced through all the same.

Captain Luna came to loom over her. "Luckily for you, you failed. Turns out you were right. One of the other dragons confirmed it. The rest of the legion have pulled back out of the marshes and lower mountains."

Elsie just lay there, gazing up at the ceiling.

"He's been moved," Captain Luna went on. "I know you lost someone in the battle in the Dales. I know you're angry, and I know you've picked off more dragons than any other hunter, but if you make another attempt on a prisoner's life, if you break the King's laws, I'll pack you off to Brevia for trial."

Elsie fought the urge to retort. Those laws had been laid down for conflict against raiders from the Splintering Isles. Against other humans.

"I understand, Captain."

The following two days passed without incident. Elsie lay flat on her back and restrained, let free only to eat a hasty meal or relieve herself, all with the indignity of another hunter guarding her the whole time. She only had herself to blame.

On the third day after attempting to slay the Prince, Elsha came by at dawn. After checking on Elsie's sling and chest, Elsha crouched down so they were at eye level and spoke softly.

"Why did you do it?"

"To kill him."

"Did you think that would help?"

"I..." Elsie hesitated, though she didn't know why. There were so many reasons. Prince Dronithir had led his soldiers ahead of the others. He was responsible for so many deaths and her own injuries. "He did this to me."

That seemed to cover all.

A shadow of doubt passed over Elsha's face, and Elsie tried to exploit it.

"You said you've seen what they do to us – how they rip us

apart. I've seen wolves show more restraint. They're dragons. They're monsters, and I've trained my whole life to kill beasts that threaten us."

The shadow on Elsha's face hung heavy, and then it passed.

"You're right," the healer said. "I've seen all of that. I've seen some of them do it... but I don't think they're all like that. I don't think *he's* like that."

Elsie blinked. She mustn't have heard correctly. "You don't think – what?"

Elsha shuffled in even closer until their faces were but a hand's distance apart. Elsie searched the girl's eyes, and despite the healer's mood, she found a brightness there. It might have been the naivety of youth, but something else mingled with it. Hope, perhaps, or yearning.

"I met him before," Elsha said, "out in the field, where the Boreacs descend into the marshes. I didn't know who he was, nor did anyone else in the patrol I was with. Like with when we found you, there had been a fight, and there were injured, and he and one other dragon were still alive."

Though Elsha spoke in hushed tones, she had a liveliness that made Elsie think she'd been dying to share this story for a while.

"He wouldn't let me come close at first, but in the end, I managed to convince him. I patched up his comrade, and while there were two of them and only a handful of us, they decided to walk away. But before they did, he thanked me... said he was surprised we'd helped an enemy."

Elsie found herself sympathizing with the Prince.

"Captain Luna told me of your loss," Elsha went on. "I lost my brother in that battle. Fools... charging head-on at the dragons."

"Don't say that—"

"What? Don't call them fools?" Grief and anger tinged Elsha's voice now. Elsie knew it well. "You've seen how strong they are. To fight them sword to sword wasn't just foolish. It was *madness*. But if we have any hope of getting out of this, we need to find dragons we can talk to."

Elsie listened. Elsie thought. Elsie didn't believe it.

"You cling to that if it gives you hope."

Elsha crept a few paces back, her face falling.

Why does she care what I think?

Without another word, Elsha got up, dusted herself off, then left the hut.

A week passed, much the same as before. Nothing changed, other than the pain in her chest subsiding by a hair and the hunter in the bed on her right at last waking up. Though Elsie was still restrained, she could talk to him, and they shared stories of the war, then older ones from when they'd kept towns safe from beasts and weren't trying to be soldiers.

"How come you're tied up like that?" he asked.

"I tried to kill a dragon in the bed next to me."

"Ah. Shame you didn't manage it."

They fell quiet after that, though Elsie felt comforted by his support.

Another day passed, and then Captain Luna returned with no less than three hunters backing her up. She untied Elsie's restraints and dragged her upright.

"Come with us."

Groaning, biting back the pain, Elsie put her trembling feet onto the floor, then shuffled along with the captain holding her left arm. The three hunters fell in behind them as they stepped outside.

In the harsh light of day, Elsie blinked and raised her one good arm against the brilliant pale sun. As her eyes adjusted, it was to a world of mountains, white up top and charcoal below, a valley filled with log buildings and crisp air salted by resinous pine.

Elsie was half dragged by Luna to one of the closer lodges. It turned out to be the hut where the critically wounded were being treated. There were fewer beds here and more healers.

Elsha was there, dabbing a cloth to a man's head. On one side, his leg was missing below the knee, and though the bandages around that wound looked fresh, Elsie felt deep within her that all was not well. Why else would she be dragged here?

Captain Hogarth's breath came in ragged wheezes. His face glistened, and his pillow was stained yellow from sweat. Luna let go of her, indicating Elsie should keep going. When she reached her captain, the air around him was sickly sweet. Laying her hand upon his, she found him burning.

Elsha rinsed out her cloth, dipped it into a basin of water, then pressed it back to Hogarth's forehead.

"We cleaned the wound as best we could," she said, "but we were too late. A rot had already got into him. There's nothing we can do."

Elsie saw it now. While the dressing around his wound was clean, dark branches of doom crept up the flesh of his thigh.

"What about that silver stuff?" Elsie asked.

"We applied needle sap when we cleaned the wound, but it can't work miracles. Giving him a small amount to drink may ease the pain, but even a little too much would kill him, and we can't spare a drop for a lost cause. I'm sorry," she said again, calm and professional. "He's wanted to speak with you. I thought you'd better come now – while you still could."

Elsha left for her other patients, and while Luna remained, she maintained a tactful distance, leaving Elsie alone by Hogarth's side.

His burning finger twitched against her hand. Struggling to keep his eyes open, Hogarth croaked, "Elsie? That you, lass?"

"I'm here."

"Ah." Hogarth lost himself in pain for some moments. "I'm on my way out... You have tae... take my place."

Lying in a dark pool of her own thoughts, she hadn't given this outcome much thought. Her first instinct was to ask if there was someone else. She yearned to ask, but she knew there was no one. Others from the marshes who might have stepped up – Grett, Haden, or Malcolm – had already fallen. Dunsten, for all his talent, was too young. And she wanted to spare Hogarth from further, needless pain. She wanted to give her captain reassurance that he could go in peace.

"Your boots will be a large pair to fill... I'll try my best."

"Good," he said, voice shaking. "Now... this dragon... listen tae Luna... we must try tae end the... end the war. He's our only hope."

For the first time since trying to kill the Prince, shame gripped Elsie.

When she failed to answer, Hogarth strained to say with urgency, "Promise me?"

"I promise."

And she meant it.

Hogarth's mouth twitched as he struggled to form a smile. He grasped her hand with what must have been the last of his strength.

"I'm sorry, lass... for everything."

It was plain he fought now for every hollow breath.

Elsie squeezed Hogarth's hand back and whispered, "Eyes wide and ahead, Captain. Eyes wide and... ahead. And good hunting."

He met her eye, managed at last to smile, then fell still. His last breath sounded like a tired sigh. Elsie held his hand for some time before placing it down at his side.

Elsha returned. The healer checked for a pulse, then gently slid Hogarth's eyes shut. As she spoke to a subordinate to note the time and date of death, Luna summoned Elsie back to her.

"Congratulations, Captain."

"I'm not sure I ever wanted it, and certainly not like this."

Luna pursed her lips and nodded.

Elise glanced over her shoulder at her former captain – and her friend, she hoped. Matters with Roy and Aleck had taken her out of the field and into a new sort of wilderness, and she'd be lying if she denied that a part of her wished to return to the days when she and Hogarth ventured forth hunting beasts together. This seemed like a whole new world now – and a worse one.

"What's been happening since we got here?" Elsie asked. "What's going on with the war?"

"I'll have a full report ready for you to read," Luna said. "If," she added with bite, "I'm assured that I won't have any *trouble* from you."

Elsie shook her head. "I made a promise. I intend to keep it."

Perhaps it was due to her own pain lessening or the fact that he was no longer within her sights, but Elsie's desire to kill the Prince seemed a waning thing.

"That is well," said Luna. "It's not up to either of us but Lord Boreac, as these are his lands, and perhaps the King, once he learns of events. I know my lord hopes to leverage the Prince as a hostage to seek a withdrawal of the dragons. For now, we keep him here and guard the passes into the mountains to ensure the dragons cannot rescue him."

That sounded far easier said than done, yet the hunters had held the dragons at bay for a while now. Why not a little longer?

Wincing, Elsie stood as straight as she could manage. "I'd like to assist in any way I can."

"You'll be of little use without that arm back," Luna said. "For now, just get better."

This time when Luna walked Elsie back to bed, it was with care rather than force.

5

THE PRISONER

After two further weeks of recovery, Elsie walked easier and regained the use of her right arm. It felt heavy at her side after so long bound in the sling, and both arm and shoulder often twinged, even in basic movements, but at least she was no longer bedbound. The first thing she'd done upon being discharged was to repair her bow's broken string.

As captain of the Cairlav hunters, her initial weeks in the role were lighter than she had a right for them to be. With the Prince a hostage, the dragons had fallen back to their position in the Dales. What would come next was anyone's guess, for so far, they had refused to open a dialogue. Some thought they would return in force to storm the mountains for their prince, believing the humans would never slay such a valuable hostage. Others thought the opposite. Rumors of dragon customs suggested they would do nothing without their leader, nor would they select a replacement on their own. Still others fell between these two peaks. The dragons would come in force again, they said, once reinforcements from the east arrived to support this one lone legion. Elsie was inclined to agree with this middling view.

Yet word of the wider world was slim, and that which arrived came slowly. With the dragons threatening lines of communication north to Brevia, messengers sent to the capital had to venture into the marshes, then take a boat across the loch. Whether this dragon king, Drakon the Fourth, had finally launched his full armada was unknown to them.

The war was in a lull, yet Elsie and Captain Luna kept their people hard at work.

Whatever may come, readying the lower mountain passes against assault seemed prudent, and the hunters of the Boreac Mountains and Cairlav Marshes worked day and night to safeguard them. They dug deep pits and filled them with spikes, hewed trees and bound the heavy trunks on steep land above the narrow pathways, raised palisades to help funnel the enemy into choke points, and laid out caltrops as fast as the smiths of the mountains could work the iron. Dragons might be tough, but the soles of their boots were still made of leather, and if caltrops could stop horses, they could stop charging dragons.

In such a traditional military exercise, they had assistance. Marshal Balliol arrived from the marshlands at the head of a few hundred spearmen, which Lord Heath had scrambled to restore out of survivors of the disastrous battle in the Dales.

Elsie wished she could pitch in, but she settled for acting as a conduit between the grizzled veteran and the hunters, overseeing the construction of the defenses while Captain Luna handled the scouting missions to keep watch over the dragons.

It all meant that Elsie spent a lot of time outside of Farlen and always with the ticking anxiety that one day she would return to find their prisoners gone and trails of blood leading into the mountains. Yet two more weeks passed, and Prince Dronithir and his two legionaries didn't cause a hint of trouble. From what the healers said, they barely spoke at all.

Still, Elsie only relied on secondhand reports, for she hadn't been allowed to visit the Prince. Despite Elsie making her promises, Elsha and Luna didn't want to present too easy an opportunity for her to break them. Yet there was a stark difference between trying to kill a restrained, injured, and half-asleep dragon and trying to kill a fully healed and alert one. Now, a month after arriving in Farlen, Elsie wouldn't stand a chance at killing the Prince. He was free of his bonds, confined and under heavy guard, but allowed the dignity of movement.

That had been done at Elsha's insistence.

The healer claimed he had to be able to move freely to recover from his injuries, so neither Luna nor Elsie could overrule her. Elsha also claimed her frequent visits to the Prince were to continue therapeutic treatments, but Elsie was growing suspicious. By the healer's own account, dragons could heal miraculously well on their own. And although the Prince might be cooperating in every regard, he was still their prisoner – and a dangerous one at that.

In time, with more trips back to Farlen, more reports, and then more gossip, this mystery began to resolve in Elsie's mind.

Every day, Elsha would enter the Prince's prison lodge, even after his wounds had healed. And every day, she would leave a little later – sometimes smiling, if the rumors were to be believed.

One evening, almost as soon as Elsie entered Farlen's tavern, Elsha pushed through the press of people to ask her how the defenses were shaping up.

"Just fine," Elsie said, entirely unsure whether they'd be fine or not. They wouldn't know until their hard work was tested, and they wouldn't get a second chance.

"That's reassuring," Elsha said. "And messengers can still go back and forth, right?"

"With a guide."

Elsie eyed the girl. It wasn't quite fair to think of Elsha as being so young, but somehow, despite all she'd seen, the girl's eyes were still bright, her skin too smooth, her braid too lush, as though she'd only tied it that day.

"Just come out and say whatever's on your mind."

"As you like." Elsha gathered herself. "We've had an idea, well, I've had an idea, which is to say—"

At that moment, Captain Luna intervened, passing Elsie a tankard of strong brown ale, then stepping in to join them. The appearance of a second captain seemed to give Elsha pause, and it showed in her face.

"Frost troll stolen your voice?" Luna asked.

"Err, no, Captain."

Another torturous pause.

Elsie took the chance to sip her ale. It was as rough as a horned crab's shell and bitter enough to make her shiver.

Elsha looked at her with some concern. "Please, Captain, I wish you wouldn't drink while your shoulder is still recovering."

Elsie looked the girl straight in the eye and took another long pull on her ale. She suppressed the shiver of disgust, but, feeling defiant, she licked her lips and said, "You had an *idea?*"

A pained look crossed Elsha's face, then she came out with it in a rush. "I think we should allow one or two dragons to come and see Dronithir."

Elsie nearly choked on her ale. Luna became, if possible, even more still.

Elsha plowed on. "A show of good faith. And Dronithir has dragons in mind who he thinks will listen—"

"Listen to what?" As before, when Elsha had spoken kindly of the Prince, Elsie couldn't believe her ears. "Listen to him inform them of our forces? Or maybe a deadline to rescue him, after which they'll be punished – ah!"

She ended with a wince as a fresh dose of pain stabbed in her chest. She waved down the healer's concern and took another drink.

Luna spoke next. "I admit I don't see the advantage."

"Dronithir wants to end this. He says his people have been

tricked into this war. This way, his men can take his wishes back to the rest of his legion. We can trust him."

Elsie was too stunned to speak.

Not only is the gossip true, it's far worse.

"Captain," Elsha said, appealing to Luna, "you've spoken with him yourself. You've heard him speak about this."

"He does have... a lot to say."

Elsie's estimation of the Boreac captain – already on the rise – shot to new heights.

"But then you must know he's serious," Elsha said.

"Healer," said Captain Luna, "I don't wish to kill him on sight, but I trust him as far as I might draw him on my bowstring. His voice is too smooth for my liking. A lot of talk of 'the Shadow' and of 'gods' and 'evil dragons' and a great guardian with a magic sword—"

"The Guardian's Blade," Elsha supplied.

"As I say, *a lot* of words... We can't track them to their source like we might a dire wolf to its lair. And in any case, such action is beyond our power to decide."

"You're both in charge here—"

Elsie could see Luna was struggling and thought a little more emotion might get the point across.

"Lord Boreac has entrusted us to safeguard his lands, not invite dragons to discover where their prince is and make us a target. Right now, the dragons don't know where he is. Right now, we have breathing room. Right now, all we have to do is hold out until Boreac's marshal can arrive with his own levies and the proper military takes charge."

She almost rattled on to say, 'Until we can go home.'

Elsha opened her mouth, then quickly closed it again, finally stuck on what to say next. She took a half step back, her eyes lost and confused as she looked between Elsie and Luna in turn.

"I don't under—" she began, then cut herself off, defeated.

"We respect your talents," Luna said. "But these matters can't be decided by us, never mind a healer. Now, do you have any other matters related to your *duties* to discuss?"

Elsha shook her head.

"Then I suggest you return to them."

Elsha nodded. "Yes, Captain."

The girl gave Elsie a quick nod as well before pushing her way through the packed tavern, leaving Elsie with a bitter taste in her mouth. Maybe it was just the ale – this stuff clung to the throat – but whether it was the drink or something else, she was left uneasy.

"I need some air," she said, then she, too, fought her way through the throng. At the door, she paused, realized she still had her tankard, felt a throb in her side, heard Elsha's admonishment, then doubled back and abandoned the drink on the closest table before heading out into the blustery night.

A chill wind whipped against her, and she'd barely taken two steps when someone hurried out of the tavern behind her.

"Captain?"

Turning, Elsie saw Elsha's dark silhouette framed in the warm doorway.

"I'm the least likely to change my mind."

"I'm not so sure." The girl joined Elsie outside. Behind her, the tavern door swung closed, sealing the orange glow away. As the night rushed back in, Elsha hurried closer.

"I know there's more at stake for you than for Captain Luna."

"What do you mean by that?"

"Please, Captain, don't treat me for a fool." Then Elsha dropped her voice conspiratorially. "I treated your wounds, remember? Cut off your leathers and shirt myself to check on your chest and shoulder – and every scuff and bruise besides. You've had a baby recently."

Her words seemed to gong in Elsie's mind, as did Lord Heath's warning.

"How did—" Elsie hissed, grabbing Elsha by the arm and

pulling her farther away from the tavern as though they might be overhead. Elsha allowed herself to be hauled a few steps, then stood her ground, and Elsie jerked back.

"Stretch marks on your lower stomach," Elsha said. "It's not exactly hard to work out."

"Have you told anyone?"

"No, I—"

"You mustn't tell anyone."

"I – I won't," Elsha said hesitantly. "But... why?"

Elsie shushed her, then took a deep, calming breath. Recovering, she said, "I can't tell you why... Just, please, will you keep it to yourself?"

"As it means so much to you."

"Promise me?"

"I promise."

Elsie nodded. "Good. Thank you."

"Of course." Elsha seemed to be waiting for something. "Could you let me go? It's starting to hurt."

Elsie realized she still had a grip on the girl's arm and let go. "Sorry."

"That's alright."

An awkwardness hung between them.

It was Elsha who broke it. "Look, all I meant by it was that I thought you'd want peace with the dragons more than most hunters. Most are younger and don't have... what you have."

The cold began to nip, and Elsie folded her arms.

"It's not that I wouldn't welcome peace," she said. "It's just that I can't... see it. And your idea isn't something I can make happen, even if I wanted to."

"Will you think on it? If you and Captain Luna were to make the case to Lord Boreac—"

"I'll think about it," Elsie cut in. "I'm afraid that's all I can do."

"Well, that's something." Elsha played with her braid, half-turned as if to leave, then stopped. "If I may ask, is it a boy or a girl?"

Elsie gulped. "A boy."

"You must miss him. I'm sorry."

"It's not your fault."

"No, but all the same. I can only imagine…"

Elsie tried to say more, but words failed her. She just nodded.

Elsha took a step away. "I'll leave you in peace, Captain. Good night."

Elsie stood and watched Elsha vanish into the darkness, then she turned in the opposite direction and started trudging through Farlen, unsure of where she was heading, just letting her feet take her where they wished to go.

There was plenty of starlight for her keen eyes to see by. She left the town behind, climbed a gentle ridge, and walked to a spot where, between the shadowed slopes of the mountains, she could see the Cairlav Marshes in the far distance. She stood and looked through the gap. Perhaps it was a trick of her mind, but she thought she could see the edge of the loch like a silver coin far away.

Guilt rose in her, guilt at not being there for her son. She was here to fight for him as much as anyone else and more than most, but still, she felt guilty. Was he waking at night, scared and alone? Was anyone tending to him the way she would?

She sniffed and rubbed at her eyes. It took a lot to fend off the irrational feeling that she should be both here fighting and back there with him. That, somehow, she should be doing both. Of the two, though, it was the pull to him that tugged harder.

Not so long ago, she'd felt fueled by a burning rage, eager to hunt dragons in the marsh. Each kill had spurred her on to more. Yet now, the fire had burnt out. Perhaps her injuries had sapped the fight out of her, but such a blaze could not have lasted forever, least of all for a whole war. This task wasn't supposed to fall to hunters. The army had learned its lesson in the Dales. Even now,

Balliol was having his militia start rudimentary training with bows. Once humanity had regrouped in full and changed tactics, the relatively small number of hunters would no longer carry such a crushing burden.

As Elsie stared at the distant silvery loch, she held on to that hope.

In due course, the new marshal appointed by Lord Boreac arrived with fresh militia from across the mountains. Marshal Berek thanked both captains for their service, then insisted they remain to help guard the lower passes until such time as the rest of the King's strength could be joined to theirs.

As promised, Elsie conveyed Elsha's request to allow the Prince to begin talks with the dragons. The marshal said no, explaining that such a decision was also above his station, but it didn't take long for Elsie to glean the truth. As a survivor of the disastrous battle in the Dales, Marshal Berek's ire ran hot. He wanted blood.

Berek dispatched messengers across the kingdom to rally aid and restarted the hit-and-run missions against dragon foraging parties. Luna led squads in person. Elsie was warier than before but obliged the Marshal, wishing only that she was fit enough to go herself. Balliol urged caution but was ignored. While they held the Prince hostage, Berek was confident they held the upper hand.

For a time, the dragons did nothing in response. Berek's raids grew bolder and the stack of legionary helmets in Farlen grew taller until, at last, he pushed his luck too far. The dragons had enough. Word came that they'd broken camp and were marching in force for the lower passes.

When the day of battle arrived, Marshal Berek boldly led his men from the front as they packed into tight ranks on the valley floor, presenting a bristling wall of spears to the enemy.

Unable to fully draw her bow, Elsie observed the battle from on high, feeling useless and overwhelmed. This was folly. Had humanity learned nothing from the Dales?

Confident as ever, the dragons poured into the valley as a sea of blinding gold. There were thousands of them. Even at a distance, the noise took Elsie aback. A hunt required stealth and precision; this was simply terror. Their roaring seemed to shake the very mountains, and suddenly all the hunters' careful traps and plans felt pitiful.

This was what Roy must have heard and felt on that terrible day.

Her mouth went bone dry. Her heart thundered in her chest.

The hardest part of all was the waiting – waiting for the dragons to advance deep enough to hurt them.

Beside her, Marshal Balliol observed the oncoming battle with equal horror. He breathed hard, and his neck turned red. He pulled at the collar of his gambeson for air, but his efforts were in vain. The material seemed wedged tight against his breastplate.

"I warned him," Balliol said, referring to Marshal Berek she knew. "All we did was provoke 'em, and for what?"

"They must not love their prince as much as we thought," Elsie said. "Otherwise they wouldn't risk his life."

"Ack, who are we tae say with this lot. But prick a bog bear enough and you're like tae get wet and bloody."

He was struggling for breath now, and his face turned red.

"Take it off," Elsie said, tapping his breastplate. "Trust me, it won't do you any good."

She expected some retort or bluster of pride, but to her surprise, the old marshal unfastened his armor and eased out of it with an exhale of relief. With renewed strength, he hefted a mace rather than a sword – the better to inflict a crushing blow against the enemy's armor.

As the dragons rushed on, relentless, undaunted, Elsie threw a glance over her shoulder. She didn't know the three hunters guarding the Prince well, for they were Boreac men; she just hoped they would have the spine to do what needed to be done.

"That's the signal!" Balliol called.

Far down the valley, a single flaming arrow shot out in an arc from beneath the cover of trees: the signal from Captain Luna to unleash the first line of their traps. Seconds later, boulders rolled and crashed out from between the pines to smash into the mass of dragons.

Elsie flexed her right hand, then drew one of the arrows from the barrel beside her. Wrapped in cloth and sitting in tar, it caught fire at once when she passed it over the brazier.

She drew back the arrow. Her shoulder screamed, and she had to let go before reaching full draw, but it was enough to send the flaming arrow high. It burned up fast, but it did its job, and more hunks of dark rock and heavy timber rolled down to smash holes in the golden host. As the dragons broke or weaved around the obstacles, they fell into hidden pits or ran heedlessly onto the caltrops covered by bracken and leaves.

Elsie sent up signals for more traps, then more, until her tar-soaked arrows were spent, yet many dragons carried on through the punishment, even bearing the first volley of arrows.

They just kept coming.

When the roaring horde met Marshal Berek's thin lines, she knew it was over.

Their only chance had been to disrupt the dragons enough to halt their momentum and cause such death and disarray as to make them rethink.

It was plain now how desperate such hopes had been. Such plans and maneuvering relied on the dragons feeling fear and breaking. But dragons were not humans. And watching them endure all this, Elsie found a strange sense of peace.

For humanity could never win. And such certainty, while terrible, did at least remove the fog of doubt and bargaining with the world. A doe cannot fend off a pack of wolves, and this was just the same.

Step by step, the spears of humanity gave ground. Arrows flew from all sides and down from vantage points, but not enough of the dragons fell, and those who did were adroitly avoided by their comrades as they pressed on. Other dragons darted up the slopes and into the trees in search of the hunters assailing them.

Feeling useless as an observer, a traitorous thought flitted through Elsie's mind. She might run. She might snatch up sacks of rations on her way and try to make it through the maze of winding, rugged passes out to the marsh. If she could make it back to Aleck, then she might...

Might what? Somehow steal him out from beneath Lord and Lady Heath and all their guards? To go where? She shook her head, managing to ward off the notion because of its absurdity.

After that, it felt easier to grip her bow and head to join the fight. Her shoulder might give out after a couple of draws, but maybe she'd take one of the beasts down with her.

Human screams rose above the roars of the dragons. A few men at the back of the wavering ranks were already fleeing, rushing back up the valley even as Elsie hastened down into it.

Then someone ran by her with such speed as to almost knock her over. It was all she could do to stay upright. Then, with dawning comprehension, she realized the rush had come from behind, and now a man was bounding downhill ahead of her like a racing deer.

Of course, it was no man. Because of her obsession with the Prince, she recognized him even from this distance – it was his frame, his height. The Prince wore rough-spun trousers and a coarse shirt, the material rippling behind him as though he trailed a white flag.

Elsie hurried after him, yelling to alert anyone she could to his presence, but no one could hear her over the din of battle, and he pushed into the rear of the humans' ranks and disappeared from view.

By the time Elsie reached the front, the howls of battle were settling, and soon the last screech of steel rang out in the suddenly silent valley.

"Let me through," Elsie insisted, pushing, shoving, gasping as her shoulder was bumped and pressed.

At the very front, she halted in awe and confusion. The dragons were kneeling. Their weapons lay strewn on the blood-soaked earth, and standing before them, the Prince held out a hand both to his own race and the humans.

Elsie looked for Berek, for Balliol, and for Luna, but she couldn't see any of them. Perhaps that was why when the Prince next spoke, he seemed to speak to her.

"We needn't keep fighting, unless you give us reason to."

Elsie gulped, and the Prince's stare turned imploring. Then, raising her hands, she said, "We don't want to fight. We don't." She turned to face the gawking human soldiers. "Back away. Come on, back away, all of you. Where are the marshals?" she called.

At length, Balliol came huffing out of the ranks of humanity to join her. He, too, seemed caught in a dream of disbelief.

"I'll take it from here, lass."

Elsie nodded, then stepped back through the ranks. She had to find Luna and start checking on the hunter casualties.

Away from the loose formation, she saw a stream of people rushing down the valley from the Farlen Pass. At their head, Elsha's long blonde braid swung wildly as she ran.

She did this.

But now wasn't the time to learn the how or why. With healers on their way, Elsie set about gathering her hunters and huntresses and finding the dead.

6

THE DIPLOMAT

Although a peace of sorts had come from it, the battle in the valley had exacted a heavy toll. Marshal Berek succumbed to his wounds two days later, leaving the Boreac soldiers once again without leadership. Captain Luna had also been found dead.

Elsie had been part of the group to find her. Luna had fallen along with a group of mixed hunters on one of the vantage points on the pine-covered slopes. They'd taken a few dragons down with them, fighting to the end with blood on their knives. At least Luna's face had been unmaimed, and had it not been for the gash across the length of her torso, she might have been resting.

And just like that, it was Elsie that all the hunters, Boreac and Cairlav alike, turned to for instruction. At least until a new Boreac captain could be appointed, for Luna's designated successor had also fallen.

When fate became cruel, it always seemed to double down.

Elsie didn't know what to do except take each day, each decision, each moment at a time. And for now, at least, there was a tentative hope that this war might end, although it was still disconcerting to see dragons moving through Farlen at their leisure.

As it turned out, not every dragon was a heavy-set bruiser. Some were lithe and fleet-footed, able to run great distances at speed. Outrunners, Elsie heard the Prince call them, and he sent these runners to take messages to his ships in the Dales and to the small garrisons he'd placed at strategic points captured during his campaign. He said he planned to sail as soon as things could be made ready.

One day, as Elsie patrolled Farlen's streets, one of these runners returned. Nothing appeared obviously amiss, but something sent a shiver down her spine. Every instinct told her something was wrong, and the way the dragon sprinted for the Prince's new lodge spoke of urgency.

Elsie gathered a dozen hunters to her, ordered one to find Balliol, then took the rest to check in on the Prince and his dragons. Before she could knock on the door, it swung open, revealing Elsha in the doorway. She looked stricken.

Fate could be very cruel indeed.

"Oh, you're here," Elsha said, flustered. "Come in."

Elsie entered, along with her eleven hunters. The Prince's previous lodgings had been his bare prison, but his new quarters now contained some of the luxuries of his homeland, hauled into the mountains by his strong kin. A table of treated dark wood gilded by some grainy gold took up a great deal of the living space. Six legionaries were hastily laying maps upon it while others consulted ledgers and documents in hushed voices.

The prince looked like himself again now that he was back in his full harness, together with the dragon-headed pauldrons and the bright red cloak, yet rather than shave like the rest of his men, he had chosen to keep the beard he'd grown as a prisoner. It was only now Elsie saw him beside his fellow dragons that the beard struck her as peculiar. She glanced at Elsha, wondering if the girl preferred him this way. Oblivious to this, Elsha called to her prince.

"She's here."

Noticing Elsie, the Prince smiled. "And with the usual show of force. How long until you believe that I mean you no further harm?"

"When you're all east of the sea again," Elsie said. She eyed the dragons pointing avidly at the maps. "I hope you haven't misplaced your ships?"

"If only," said the Prince. He stood collected, hands behind his back. "You needn't worry too much, but there's been a development that will delay our departure. Another legion has landed in the Dales. My outrunner met one of their own while scouting."

Elsie failed to see the issue, and that made the shiver down her spine spasm again.

"So order them to stand down and head home."

"Ah, I'm afraid that's the harder part. Any other legion and I might be able to, but this one is led by the Lord Guardian. Many are part of his elite Light Bearers and are fiercely loyal to him and the Way of Light, more so than even to my father."

Elsie couldn't help but agree with Luna's sentiment. The Prince used a lot of words.

"I'm also afraid they aren't in the finest of moods," the Prince went on. "It seems other ships under the Guardian's care were sunk or scattered by your human fleets. As such, they are keen to extract their measure of blood in turn. But, as I say, I wouldn't worry too much."

"Sounds like we ought to. You just said that this... *Guardian* isn't beholden to you."

"That may be so, but he's a good dragon – a good man. He's served my father well for decades and even taught me swordcraft and scripture as a boy. His purpose is to safeguard our race against further encroachment of the Shadow, the corrupting power that claimed our Black Dragon kin long ago. Norbanus – that is to say, the Lord Guardian – deemed that humanity had become corrupted by the Shadow, but he is clearly mistaken. When I go to him, when I explain and show him his error, he'll understand the folly."

Again, there was an awful lot said there that Elsie struggled to follow. However, before she could enquire further, Elsha asked with concern, "You're going to see him?"

The Prince faced her. "Of course."

"To... talk?" Elsie asked.

The Prince turned back to Elsie. "We dragons can talk as well as we fight when we want to."

"When are you going?" Elsha asked.

Elsie took a step back. "Perhaps I should leave you two to discuss—"

"Stay," the Prince urged, then took Elsha's hand in his. "I would have you come with me, if you are willing. You helped me to understand the truth of your kind, and I'm sure you can clear that same fog from his mind."

For once, the girl looked uncertain. She half-opened her mouth, but the words caught in her throat. Elsie thought that was quite the thing. Elsha had been certain enough in her prince to drug his guards with silver needle sap and then set him free to stop the battle. She supposed even bright-eyed youths had their own wariness thresholds, even if they were farther out from shore. Elsie remembered being even younger than Elsha was now and telling Roy they couldn't just run away together: though she loved him, such a thing was too frightening.

I should have just said yes.

Dragging herself back to the moment, to the Prince's lodge, Elsie tried to reassure Elsha. "You're allowed to say no."

Elsha started as though she'd forgotten other people were in the room. "No – I mean, yes, I... I'll go. Of course I will. Anything that might help heal the hurt between our peoples."

The Prince beamed.

"You're sure?" Elsie asked.

"I am, Captain. I'll save countless more lives this way than by healing one wound at a time." She met Elsie's eyes with great deliberation. "If we do this right, then every *newborn child* will never need to fear again."

Wouldn't that be something?

Though it was impossible, Elsie tried to forget for a moment that she had a child she worried about. If she didn't have Aleck, would Elsha's words have hit her as hard? Perhaps not. As the acting captain of the Boreac hunters, Elsie could deny the girl and keep her here. Then again, if there was a chance? Plus, Elsha wanted to go, and the Prince seemed assured that all would go smoothly.

"When will you leave?" Elsie asked.

"As soon as we can," said the Prince. "I was about to order my legionaries to return to our ships, but under the circumstances, they ought to remain encamped outside these mountains. I trust that is acceptable?"

"It is," Elsie said.

Not that we could do much to prevent it.

"Wonderful. A small party will travel swifter than a whole legion. With luck, we'll be back in the golden city before the season turns."

He was speaking more to Elsha again, so Elsie cleared her throat. "Do you require anything more?"

"Nothing," the Prince said, still holding the healer's hand. "I have all that I need."

Elsie left with her hunters and made it halfway down the road when Balliol came bustling toward her with the hunter she'd sent to find him. She and Balliol then made for the hunter's lodge and retreated into a quiet corner. Their only company in the nook was the stuffed body of a blood hawk that hung suspended from the ceiling, its beak alarmingly red against its body of gray feathers. As Balliol paced, his head passed just under the hawk's long talons.

"Another legion always had tae come," he said, scratching at his beard. "We can be thankful it's only the one."

Elsie couldn't help but laugh, though the sound emerged choked and strained. Balliol huffed a laugh of his own, then fell serious again.

"Best be ready for the worst, I say," he said. "What with this truce, I was thinkin' of heading back tae Torridon anyway. Check in on whether those promised reinforcements ever showed up."

Elsie ran her hands down her face, then shrugged. "We can't fight them. You saw what would have happened to us out there."

"I did, aye. But I also dinnae see what else there's tae do? It's give it a go or roll belly up and be done wi' it."

That was true enough, and Elsie found herself nodding again.

"I'll stay here then," she said, chewing on the words. "Try to... well, something. And Marshal, I know you've had your reasons to think less of me, and I don't expect that to change, but, as you're going home, might you check in on—"

He clamped a meaty hand down on her good shoulder. "Aye, lass. I will."

That he didn't make a meal of it felt oddly touching.

"Thank you."

"Don't thank me yet," he said, heading for the door. "Chin up," he barked by way of encouragement. "If the Prince feels so sure, he must have good reasons. All the same, stay sharp while I'm gone."

"I shall, and you keep your eyes wide and ahead as well."

The Prince, Elsha, and a band of dragon legionaries set off as planned, leaving Farlen quieter than it had been in some time. Only a handful of dragons remained to act as liaisons, and most of them were outrunners. Elsie would occasionally inquire for news or insight from the surly legate in charge, but this dragon didn't share his prince's love of talking.

Elsewise, little changed for the hunters and soldiers while they waited. Lord Boreac sent a decree that Elsie should maintain her captaincy of both sets of hunters to create a united force until the crisis was over. Elsie feigned a smile and inwardly cursed the lord, who still hadn't deigned to descend from his secure manse high up in the snowy range.

As the wait turned from days into weeks, Elsie wondered whether Elsha's presence had slowed the dragons down. She pictured the Prince carrying Elsha in his arms to keep up the pace. Perhaps two weeks wasn't so long. Elsie still lacked a clear understanding of how fast the dragons could move and for how long. The runners were exceptions, carrying next to nothing and wearing only light tunics rather than the heavy armor the Prince and his men wore.

As it happened, the wait became long enough that Marshal Balliol returned to the lower passes first, bringing reinforcements like he had hoped. Back in their quiet nook of the hunter's lodge, he slumped into a chair opposite Elsie and blew on his red hands to fend off the numbing cold. Elsie put some more wood on the fire and poked at it. She'd grown accustomed to the chill of Farlen by now, even as the days grew shorter.

As she sat back down, she thought the old marshal looked trimmer around the waist, though she held her remark and allowed him to catch his breath and warmth. While she waited, she felt aware of the presence of the blood hawk gazing down at them in judgment.

Between sighs of relief and rubbing his hands, Balliol at last said, "Got good news."

"Oh?" Elsie said in genuine surprise. "I'm ready to hear it."

Balliol leaned forward and started counting off with his fingers. "Lads from the Crescent, the Crown Lands, and even some from the Hinterlands. Plenty of them. Word's been getting around that the marshlands and the mountains have been givin' the dragons a thrashing."

Elsie snorted.

"It's spread some hope. Not sure the chevaliers in Brevia are much pleased by it, but as they arsed up already, they can't get too crusty over it."

Elsie looked about as though someone was missing. "Where are the Crescent and Hinterland captains?"

They'd have more experience than her – they could take over.

"They'll still in the Crescent and the Hinterlands, I should think."

Used to nodding by now, that was what Elsie did. So that was her fate. No replacement would come. As Captain, she'd be here until the end of things, or the end of her.

"How bad has it been without us keeping the marshes safe?"

She was braced for reports of savage wolf attacks, horn crab numbers overrunning prime fishing and eel pools, and cusith stealing babies from the cradle.

"Ah, got some good news there an' all. There's much less tae worry about than usual. The wolves and bog bears seem to be keeping to themselves or have cleared off. And barely anyone's heard a cusith cry for months. A great pack of 'em were seen heading into the eastern marsh, and there's been nothing since."

"That's good news, is it? A massive pack of cusith now unaccounted for."

Balliol scratched at his tangled hair and shrugged. "If they ain't causing trouble, I'd say it's a win."

That was true enough. She didn't have the capacity to worry over what the beasts might be up to or what might be needed to deal with them in the future, and the desire for the real news she'd been dying to hear now demanded to be satisfied. Through an effort to control that desire, her words came out a little higher than usual.

"How's Aleck?"

Balliol didn't answer immediately. He blew on his hands and rubbed them again, though their color was back to normal. At length, he said, "Aye, he's good, lass. Right wee fighter. Good set o' lungs on him."

"You saw him?"

"Er, briefly."

"That's... that's good." She bit her lip, and her eyes stung. When had she last slept soundly through the night? "Did Lord Heath have any message for me?"

"Ah, no. I asked, but..." Balliol trailed off, rummaging in one of his travel sacks, perhaps to avoid meeting her eye.

Despite the sting of Lord Heath's lack of decency, Elsie was touched by Balliol's plain regret. He seemed to have softened on her. There must be some truth to what folk said about soldiers and the bonds of battle.

With a grunt, Balliol concluded his search, emerging with a tiny, loosely covered bundle.

"I managed tae get this for you."

He handed the bundle over. Elsie took it, lost as to what it might be. Then, between the folds of cloth, she saw something pale blue. Her heart skipped a beat, then she pulled out Aleck's blue swaddling suit.

Elsie didn't know how to feel. It was too much. He had already outgrown it? Well, of course that would happen. It was inevitable. He'd grow, learn, play, take his first steps, speak his first word – but what word would that be? And who would he say it to?

"I'd appreciate it if you didnae mention this to anyone," Balliol said. "I wasn't exactly given it, if you get me."

Dazed, it took Elsie a moment to 'get him,' but she nodded. Always she nodded.

"I'll leave you be then, lass."

He got up.

"Marshal," she said. "Thank you."

He left, and Elsie turned her full attention to the blue suit between her fingers. It felt so soft. All thoughts of dragons and princes and guardians and everything melted from her mind. She made sure she was alone, then brought Aleck's old suit close and inhaled through the fabric. A flood of memories rushed to the surface, all of him. The scent was warm, delicate, sweet, and, above all, soothing.

That night, Elsie walked out to the ridge outside town where the marshes could be glimpsed between the craggy blue outlines of distant slopes. Clouds blocked the stars that night, so she couldn't see the loch's surface, but she stayed for a while and looked anyway.

Days after Balliol's return, there was still no news of the Prince's party. Even the sour-looking legionary had something to say about that, and outrunners were dispatched east into the Dales to seek what information they could.

Elsie wasn't sure what she expected to hear, but she certainly hadn't expected the Prince to return with one of the runners on his own, bloodied and carrying a strange shield, yet that was what she discovered upon emerging from the lodge as an ochre sun lowered behind the peaks.

The Prince dragged himself into the center of Farlen, slowing just outside the tavern, then came to a halt, looking down at nothing. Townsfolk emerged to stare and whisper, and the icy tingle down Elsie's spine trickled colder than ever.

"What's happened?" she asked.

The Prince looked at her with glazed eyes. He didn't answer. Instead, he threw his shield down. A strange, bright yellow symbol was emblazoned upon it, a sword cutting through a sun of spiraling lines. Next, the Prince's crimson cloak fell to cover it. Piece by piece, he started stripping his armor while his glazed stare tilted up toward the higher mountains.

Elsie approached with her hands raised. "You're clearly upset. Come inside and tell us what happened."

She looked imploringly at the outrunner who had returned with him, but the dragon looked just as confused as she was and a lot more concerned. Behind him, coming through the entrance to the town, at least a score of legionaries were approaching at a run, calling for their prince.

But he ignored them. It was like he didn't hear them at all.

"My fault," he mumbled to no one. "He must be stopped... wrong... tricked..."

The new legionaries rushed to encircle their prince, trapping him and Elsie with their bodies. A few whistling hunter calls rang out as well.

"Do nothing," Elsie called. "Everything is fine. He's clearly ill."

By now, the Prince had stripped down to his shirt and trousers and began to advance barefoot at a snail's pace, still fixated by the mountains.

"I hear you," he said vacantly. "Yes... I shall come."

With that, he sprang forward, pushing past his dragons and racing faster than Elsie had ever seen a dragon run, faster even than when he had hurtled to stop the battle in the valley.

Caught off guard, his fellow dragons seemed sluggish by comparison, and though some gave chase, the Prince outstripped them all, disappearing along the winding road leading into the mountains. Within the hour, the other dragons had traipsed back into Farlen, breathless and defeated. They'd lost all trace of him.

And so it was that Elsie spent the following days scouring the surrounding hills, paths, valleys, and settlements for signs of the Prince's whereabouts. She relied on the Boreac hunters, for they were more accustomed to the terrain. Legionaries insisted on joining the search, and Elsie allowed one per group but no more. To her surprise, they agreed without protest.

While tracking the Prince, she tried to glean what information she could about what had happened to him and his delegation. His dragons were unsure. No one else had returned, and the Prince had only given them hasty orders, then rushed off.

Yet given his state of mind, Elsie concluded the worst. His hadn't been the actions of a person acting to save someone they loved – he seemed gripped in a delirium only grief could bring on. She recognized the look of it, the smell of it, and that made her pity the Prince. She'd thought Elsha was the bright-eyed one of the pair, but he'd meant every word he'd said.

During the hunt, a young Boreac hunter in Elsie's group found the Prince's tracks, and they followed them high enough to touch the snow, yet here the prints vanished altogether. It made no sense. It wasn't possible. One step they were there, plain and deep in the snow, and the next, all was as pristine as white velvet.

He was simply gone.

The dragons didn't like that at all, but eventually they accepted there was no trail to follow, and Elsie called off the hunt.

That night, she and Balliol sat together again, this time in a dim corner of the tavern. The atmosphere was tense, spirits were low, and both captain and marshal nursed their bitter drinks.

"Coward," Elsie muttered darkly. "If he wanted to end things, he should've fought this other dragon lord. Instead, he's left us to face the end without him."

"Ack, we don't—"

But Balliol stopped himself there. Even as a dragon, there was no way the Prince would survive for long without food, clothes, or shelter. As if to excuse his pause, Balliol drank, made a grunt of revulsion, then pushed the tankard aside.

"Piss water this, ain't it?"

Elsie nodded. "It's no Crescent Nectar."

"Damned place. I'd give a lot for a sweet tankard again afore the end of all this."

Elsie was about to ask what would come next when several dragons thumped up to their table, led by their erstwhile liaison, Legate Marius. His expression was as grim as ever, and his voice grimmer still.

"We must talk."

"I'm sorry," Elsie said in anticipation, "but the trail's gone cold."

"We are aware. We must talk about how to deal with the Guardian Norbanus."

Elsie blinked. "Sorry, I must have misheard you. That sounded like you think we're going to fight him?"

"We are," Marius said. He seemed entirely unmoved by the notion.

"How exactly can we do that?"

"Alongside us. Before he rushed up the valley to this town, Prince Dronithir's last orders to us were to engage the Lord Guardian's legion and defend humanity at all costs."

"And you're happy to do that?" Elsie asked.

Under the table, Balliol kicked her. She grunted but took his point.

"What the good captain means tae say is that we're extremely grateful for yer assistance."

"We are," Elsie said, and she appreciated their astonishing devotion to their prince, even if to a fault. The Prince had seemed half-possessed when he'd stumbled into Farlen, clearly not in his right mind. Had any of her old captains issued orders in such a state, she'd have been happy to ignore them. In the here and now, however, she was glad the dragons acted differently. As much as they unnerved her, if they would fight alongside humans, they all had a damned sight better chance of success.

Yet saying they would work together and actually doing so proved entirely different things. Elsie and Balliol spoke of the virtues of bringing the enemy into the lower valley again, with all the traps, but this time, the dragons would hold the line. That seemed the best way to utilize their lower numbers. The Prince's legion had inflicted devastation on humanity, but they had suffered losses, while the Guardian's legion was full and fresh.

But Marius and his legionaries would hear none of it. Norbanus had been told of what had happened in the battle in the valley and would not be led into another trap like that so easily. Besides, holding choke points and springing ambushes were wholly foreign concepts to them.

They proposed various means of meeting the enemy on the open field, but Elsie thought each plan madder than the last. Bullish confidence alone wouldn't be enough, and darkly, she wondered whether the legionaries saw their new human allies as disposable meat shields, soaking the enemy's attention while they did the real work.

We're going to argue ourselves into defeat, Elsie thought.

She was close to the point of despair when, one day, the Prince emerged like a ghost out of the wilderness.

He came at dawn.

Elsie hadn't slept well and so was up and out in the thin blue light when she saw him stepping softly into town. He made no sound and moved with a grace no human ever could. Far from bone thin or blackened from frost, the Prince looked – well, there was no other way to describe it – resplendent.

He seemed to *glow*.

Elsie rubbed her eyes, wondering whether she was dreaming, but the chill nipping at her skin was all too real.

The Prince looked around serenely, and with so few people out at this hour, his eyes quickly met Elsie's own. He smiled as though they were old friends and ushered her and then everyone else closer. Hunters, goat herders up for the morning milk, night watchmen ending their shift, and even bakers emerged as though drawn to a warm fire on a winter's night.

Closer now, Elsie noticed something new about him besides his otherworldly pull. A sword hung from his waist in a plain sheath. Only the grip stood out to her, wrapped in black and gold cloth. When the Prince touched it, the world around him seemed to draw breath.

Then, still smiling, he spoke.

"We have much work to do."

7

THE CHAMPION

Away from Farlen, upon the ridge where the marshes could be seen, Elsie sat on a smooth-topped boulder and dangled her feet over its edge. She'd forgotten how vibrant the marshes were on a clear day like this. Pink and red flora seemed to float upon the distant morass.

Her breath steamed as she recovered from a hasty climb, and despite the cold, she tugged at her collar. The Boreac hunters often quipped that the mountains had two seasons – winter and lesser winter. They were heading deep into proper winter now. She'd borrowed one of their fur-lined cloaks, and it was so good at its job she wanted to rip the damn thing off half of the time.

From behind her, she heard heavy boots crunching over small stones. She steeled her nerves and clenched her jaw before turning to face him.

The Prince was back in his full armor, his red cloak flowing behind him like a mane. Unlike her, he was not short of breath.

"May I join you, Captain?"

She raised her eyebrows.

"I'd like to talk."

Elsie bit her lip, then resigned herself. "Sure." She shuffled along the boulder and patted the space beside her. If he was surprised by the gesture, he didn't show it and came to sit with her as though it were perfectly ordinary. She expected him to ask her something, but he remained quiet and stared across the landscape as the breeze rustled around them.

At last, he did speak. "I'm told you come up here often."

"Some nights I slip away when I need to clear my head."

"You're from there," he said, nodding toward the marshlands.

She nodded as well.

"It's a wild, harsh sort of land. Striking to behold."

Elsie let him go on, wondering where he was going with this.

"Across the sea to the east, we dragons live in a city of gold, in a warm land of plenty. The earth is level, rich, and well-tilled. Fruits swell with sweet juice throughout the year. Most of our kind know little of the world beyond."

"Are you trying to say you came here to explore?"

"No. I came to conquer. I came to earn my inheritance. Among my race, much is determined by our prowess in war. Maybe that is our great flaw."

Elsie's instinct was to snap back, to tell him of a few more flaws, but instead, she found herself saying, "Humans fight a lot, too."

They fell quiet again, and Elsie looked back out to the marshes. There rose an urge deep inside her to shuffle along the boulder, just an inch away from the dragon. It wasn't fear, not true fear to chill the spine and race the heart. More a gentle discomfort. Perhaps it was just knowing what he was capable of, like sitting beside a trained war hound, knowing what it could do if its training just *slipped*.

"Do you have a family there?" he asked, pointing to the marsh.

She started, wondering if Elsha had divulged her secrets. She decided she hadn't. The Prince wasn't one to mince his words. If he knew, he wouldn't have asked.

That still left a problem. How should she answer? Lord Heath would have her say nothing at all. And she'd promised to do just that.

"Sort of," she said. Then, curter than she intended, she asked, "What does it matter to you?"

"We're to stand side by side in the coming fight, and I like to know my senior officers."

"I'm one of your officers, am I?"

She could see the regret on his face. "A poor choice of words, but the intent is genuine. I like to know what drives those around me. With dragons, I've heard it all, but you and your kind are largely unknown to me. If we survive this, then one day I'll be King, and I'd like our people to be able to live in peace with one another. Perhaps even become allies."

"Peace would be good."

He smiled and then waited expectantly.

Elsie supposed speaking vaguely couldn't hurt. This dragon prince wouldn't contribute to the gossiping nobles in Brevia. Sighing, she said, "I have a son. Just a son."

"So you came to fight for him?"

"I came to fight because I had little choice, but yes, for him. And for vengeance."

"Vengeance," he echoed bitterly. Then, more gently, he asked, "You lost someone?"

She nodded.

"Ah... I am sorry. Did he take part in the first... *battle?*" He ended as though unsure of the word.

She closed her eyes and nodded. Always she nodded.

"Those men were brave," the Prince said.

"Don't—"

"I've never felt worse in my whole life. True victories, those hard-won against the real threats to the world, are never so easy. We sailed to combat the Shadow, and soon thousands lay dead at our feet, but all we'd achieved was the slaughter of those weaker than ourselves. You have every right to hate us for that, to hate me. I hate myself for falling prey to such madness."

A pinch of pity rose inside Elsie, but she ably swatted it aside. Her grief and anger and guilt roiled again, and a bit of it escaped her in the form of a lone, hot tear. She opened her eyes and let it fall.

"If you felt that way," she said, "why did you keep going?"

"I'm able to articulate all of it with the benefit of hindsight, but at the time, I think I was too confused to do anything other than carry on. And then we soon encountered your kind. Hunters. Skilled in stealth and the bow. Bog devils, we called you. You reminded us of the magics the Black Dragons employ with darkness and shadow, so we thought Norbanus was right after all. Maybe that first battle had been a ruse to lull us into overconfidence. So, I ordered caution until we could learn more. But, if I'm being honest, the more we encountered you, the more I began to doubt."

"Why was that?"

"Because we could smell the fear on you. It was so strong. Our real enemies don't carry a scent like that."

Elsie blinked – had she heard that right?

"You don't literally mean that, do you?"

Now it was his turn to look confused. "I mean what I say. Dragons can smell fear. It smells sweet to us, and sometimes, the air was so sweet in the marshes it was sickly."

As bizarre as that sounded, it made sense to Elsie, given all the sniffing the dragons did as they stomped around. And how the dragons always seemed to find them whenever a cusith howled within earshot. It had been fear. It smelled *sweet*. Small wonder Elsie felt uneasy sitting so close to a dragon.

Queasy as it made her, she appreciated that he was being open. He was trying, and she was determined to do the same.

"Well, if you want to learn what humans are like, being afraid is top of the list. Everything from death to what some snooty lords in the capital might think of your son's choice of bride." The Prince looked puzzled, but before he could ask more, Elsie hurried on. "Can dragons feel fear?"

"It's rare, but we do. I'd thought I knew what it felt like, but I recently got a taste of the real thing... and it was overwhelming. If that's how you feel a lot of the time, I deem it a hard existence."

"Is that why you were always out with your dragons in the marshes? Because you weren't afraid?"

"Leading from the front is expected of our king, so I must act the part, even as a prince. How can we demand dragons march into danger if we won't go ourselves?" He seemed to consider something, then sniffed hard and carried on. "Even had I known the danger Norbanus posed, I still would have gone to see him, but I wouldn't have let—"

His next words stuck in his throat. He flexed his hand and breathed a little harder.

There it was again. That pesky flicker of pity inside her.

She'd come to learn the contours of the tragic events of his diplomatic mission. How this Guardian hadn't been impressed with the Prince's notion of making peace; how he claimed the corruption of humanity had rubbed off on him; how Elsha had been seen as the heart of this corruption; and how she'd had to be cut free to 'save' him.

"Did you really have no idea?" Elsie asked.

"None. I never dreamed he'd do... that. Not after making the case myself. Only the King has both the authority and the raw power to challenge the Guardian, but my father's slow decline has allowed Norbanus to act unchecked for too long. I see now how dangerous that is. Norbanus is too blinded by his own righteousness ever to question himself, and anyone else who dares is a blasphemer. He must be stopped, or I fear your whole race will be in peril."

Elsie could feel the pressure of it all physically pressing upon her, grinding her against the rock. Even if they got through this war, the fact remained that dragons were frighteningly powerful. Humanity would always live in fear.

"What's to stop all of this from happening again?"

"Nothing can be made certain, but when I'm King, I shall take measures to reduce the chance as best I can. I have some ideas – some are of deterrence, and some are to reform things east of the sea. The details can come later. Right now, we must make sure I get that chance."

His tone was calm and his words measured, so perhaps it was just Elsie's unease and bias, but she thought she saw something hard in his eyes that belied the softness of his speech. But no sooner had she glimpsed whatever it was than it vanished. Perhaps it had been only the shadow of a passing cloud.

"Seems you have it all worked out," she began tentatively. "I can't believe I'm admitting this, but it was very fortunate for us all that Elsha met you in the marsh."

"She told you of that, did she?"

"After I tried to kill you."

"Which time?"

"The second, after *you* nearly broke me in half by throwing me."

"In self-defense."

She scoffed. "Alright, fine. As I said, it was just as well for that chance encounter. When Elsha told me her tale, she was whispering, but I got the feeling she wanted to shout about it from the mountaintops... For what it's worth, she must have felt something for you even then."

Elsie tapped her heels off the rock a few times, feeling awkward and unsettled in equal measure. Part of her still hated the Prince, hated what he'd done. Another part was too weary to hold on to such poison. And yet another burned to know what had happened to him – to understand. With all the talk of gods and magic swords, just how much of it was real?

"What really happened to you when you ran off? How did you survive?"

"I thought I had explained that already. The gods spoke to me, and I answered them."

"Yes, but what does that mean?"

"It's hard to remember, actually," he said, squinting as though trying to relive the experience. "It all feels jumbled now, but at the time, it felt as sharp as steel."

"And the gods gave you... that?" Elsie asked, pointing to the pommel of his sword poking out from under his cloak.

"They saw fit to grant me use of it. For now, at least."

The Prince pulled back his cloak to reveal the sword in full. It looked plain, considering the origins he claimed for it. The cross-guard was plain steel, the pommel round. Only the quality of the black and gold cloth on the grip seemed fine.

"And it has... magic powers?"

"It has granted me access to magic. Those who understand this force call it Cascade energy. I finally appreciate what they mean by it now."

"And can this *magic*, can it—"

"It can't."

It was as if a fist had taken hold of her heart.

"You don't even know what I was going to ask."

"I do, because it was the first thing I asked. It cannot be done. They're gone, Captain."

She felt sick, felt foolish for even daring to hope for a second. Another tear leaked out and rolled down the other side of her face. Wiping it away, she caught the Prince's eye and was reassured not to glimpse the hardness again.

"I keep hoping I'm just a temporary captain. So call me Elsie."

"Very well. And you may call me Dronithir."

She made the weakest of smiles. To be bonded by a sense of loss seemed a sour thing, but better that than bitter hatred.

"Alright then, Dronithir. I hope your magic sword is enough to best this Guardian."

"You leave worrying about fighting him to me. As for the rest, let's just hope he, his legate, and his prefects take the bait."

Dronithir's return had silenced Legate Marius's notions of fighting in the open field. Thankfully, they'd come up with an alternative.

"If he's half as arrogant as he sounds," Elsie said, "I think he'll take the bait."

Feeling she'd had enough emotionally grueling discussions for one day, she got to her feet, jumped down from the boulder, and took a few steps toward Farlen before turning back.

"So, do you need to know more about me, or are we good?"

The Prince smirked, rose to his feet, and inclined his head. "Well enough. I'm glad we found this time. I fear there won't be many opportunities once we enter the marsh." With that, he did something peculiar and extended his hand toward her, though his fingers were spread wide like frog feet. "Elsha said your people like to shake hands when in agreement."

Elsie smiled for real this time. She extended her hand and made a point of showing how her fingers were together and her palm slightly cupped. When he mimicked her, she took his hand and squeezed as hard as she could, even though he probably wouldn't feel a thing from her meager strength.

A twinge ran back up to her shoulder. Even after all this time, it hadn't entirely returned to normal, much like her shapeshifting feet after the pregnancy. But when she spoke to the Prince, she hid all trace of her discomfort.

"Let's go hunting together, Dronithir."

8

THE FIGHT

Armed with daring and boldness, Elsie at last left the mountains along with the bulk of their combined hunter forces, their human soldiers – whether rag-tag militia or men-at-arms – and Dronithir's battered legion.

They first marched north and east toward the coast, where Dronithir's ships lay anchored off the shore. All reports suggested Norbanus hadn't moved since establishing a foothold on the peninsula and would be content to wait until more legions arrived. Time was now of the essence, and Norbanus would have to be baited into a confrontation.

Dronithir ordered his ships to set sail and sink Norbanus's own.

When the ships returned, their numbers were fewer, but they brought both good and bad news. The good news was that Norbanus's galleys and transports had been taken by surprise, and the majority sunk or severely damaged. The bad news was that reinforcements had been disembarking even as the attack took place. About half a legion managed to land, swelling Norbanus's ranks.

The next reports confirmed that Norbanus had broken camp and was now marching west at great speed. Well, they'd wanted to provoke him. If only they'd struck sooner. At least the attack had prevented Norbanus from doubling his numbers, but, all the same, his previously good odds now seemed all but guaranteed.

Bold and daring the scrappy coalition might be, but they'd need a stroke of immense good fortune to find success. Elsie hoped that those gods Dronithir spoke of were real and were really on his side.

Dronithir ordered the crews off the ships to join his ranks, then the coalition headed west to enter the Cairlav Marshes and begin the crawl across the narrow strips of wet ground between lagoons.

Elsie had offered up their intended destination. Near Loch Minian's south-eastern inlet was an area large enough to host their battle lines. It was no hill, nor even a hummock, but elevated enough for the water to drain from it on all sides, making it something of an island. Cloaked by tall reeds and the gnarled, twisted marsh trees, Elsie didn't think their assailants would understand how poor the ground was for anyone attacking. Some of the pools could swallow a grown man whole in their blue-green jaws.

Once they arrived, Dronithir paced the length and width of the island, counting out his strides. He did this three times, then returned to confer with Elsie and Marshal Balliol.

"It'll do," he said. "But to cover the full ground, my dragons will only be three ranks deep."

"Even made o' gold, that's a thin line," Balliol said. "What would you have all my spearmen do if not join the ranks?"

"I'm trying to spare your men from—"

"Put them in," Elsie said. "We're not here to be protected."

"Very well. Have your most stout-hearted spearmen take the center. My dragons shall hold the flanks, then fold in upon the enemy once they've overcommitted. Gods smile on us – we shall win the day."

He started pacing again before barking orders to legionaries, who saluted and hurried off to fulfill them.

"The man can talk, can't he?" Balliol said in an undertone. As Elsie gave an appreciative chuckle, Balliol groaned and rubbed his eyes. "It's no' a nice place tae die, lass. Hope it's over quick."

By the time they'd brought up all their baggage, the western end of the island had become laden with a wall of supplies. But rather than act as a barrier, it served to wall them in. They'd win or they'd die.

"We shall sleep under the stars," Dronithir told his dragons, who were used to orderly rows of clean white tents. "Smile to the night, for N'weer will be watching us."

And so, every man, woman, and dragon slept on the damp ground.

And they waited.

Two days passed at a torturous pace. Elsie checked their arrow supplies so many times she had to remove six splinters from her fingers. Balliol coped the best, puffing on a thin pipe and exchanging stories with some of the older men of the battles of their youth, of the dispute between the Dalelanders and the King in Brevia, and of patrolling the coasts against raiders from the Splintering Isles. Better days, they said. Elsie supposed that, if she had to pick, fighting men was preferable to fighting dragons.

Dronithir fared worst of all. His pacing became relentless, and he hardly slept. Elsie suspected he didn't sleep at all. With his new sword in hand, he didn't appear to tire, and in the dark, his eyes faintly glowed. Frustrated, he summoned half a dozen squads of his dragons and gave loud instructions for them to head east and ensure Norbanus was lured to the site of battle.

"We must draw him out. We cannot risk him becoming wary."

Panicked, Elsie rushed to his side. "Dronithir, I have hunters out there scouting. Your dragons might give away their positions."

The glint in his eyes dimmed. He seemed to recognize the rashness but remained determined. "Go," he told his men, "and if you come across the hunters, tell them to fall back. We don't want them caught out."

Elsie wished to argue the point, wanted to remind him that her patrols wouldn't be easy to spot, that his dragons would move slower, for they didn't know the way, but she caught that glimpse of hardness in his eyes again and decided to act instead.

Rounding up every Cairlav hunter and huntress left, she readied them to join her in ensuring their comrades made it safely back. The rest – hunters of the Boreacs in their white leathers, the Crescent hunters in yellow, and those from the Hinterlands in stony gray – she ordered to remain and assist in the battle. All lacked camouflage for the terrain, apart from the remnants of the Daleland hunters with their green and brown leathers, but they weren't experienced in navigating the marshes, and she would need speed if they were to succeed.

At the edge of the island, she stopped to put on her hard green cap, bunching up her hair before wiggling the cap down to a snug fit. She rolled her tight shoulder, then closed her eyes, listening to the haunting winds whisper through the reeds, smelling the tang of the water, feeling the damp air against her face.

The others readied behind her. Time to go.

Her hand moved instinctually.

Quiver, feathers, string.

Bow in hand, she blew lightly on her whistle, then led her hunters east into the marsh, moving as swiftly and quietly as green ghosts. Their lighter frames and clothing would allow them to outstrip Dronithir's dragons by hopping onto soft ground that couldn't take the weight of dragon muscle and armor.

An hour later, Elsie heard the first whistle not borne of the wind, and she replied with two keen blasts. Through such exchanges, they found the first group of Cairlav hunters, and another signal from the south told of another group being located.

The reports were promising. Norbanus's legion had entered the marshes and were making their way west, following what Elsie hoped would be an obvious trail from their recent march. By all accounts, they were getting close – Dronithir's dragons would surely encounter them and rouse them into a final push. The Prince would have his battle.

Following further whistling, each group was brought together. One pair emerged from the north red-faced and breathless.

"Captain?" the hunter said, clearly not expecting to see her.

"What's the matter?"

"Dragons," he said, still trying to catch his breath. His companion was bent double.

"Good," Elsie said. "That's what we want."

"North," the hunter gasped. He coughed, then seemed to regain himself. "A line of them moving away from the rest of the host."

"How many?"

"Hard to say. Maybe a hundred?"

"Sounds like a flank," someone offered.

"There's another approach to the island from that side," said another.

Yes, Elsie thought, *but how would the dragons know that?*

She counted the hunters again. Fifty-six. Not fifty-eight.

Elsie blew on her whistle, but no more replies sounded. Whether prisoners or traitors, the missing pair was gone. And whether willingly offered or extracted at the end of a knife, some of their knowledge had gone with them.

"Captain?" someone asked.

Another hissed, "Shhhh."

They fell silent. Even the pair fighting for breath held theirs for a moment.

Steel cut through the thick air and reeds. Boots splashed. Many voices grunted to form a chant. Norbanus's host was grinding closer.

Elsie thought fast. Dronithir and Balliol wouldn't be able to turn a portion of their forces to face north without conceding precious ground for the enemy to get a toehold in their flank. She also knew that even one hundred dragons puncturing their formation would be like a stiletto thrust between two ribs.

"We must head off this flanking force," she decided aloud. "Even if we only weaken it. Come now, quick and quiet as we can."

There was no whistle this time, just words passed to those behind.

North they went, taking the more dangerous, narrow route to cut across the enemy's path. They made it with perhaps minutes to spare. Already the dragons were heading south for the island, splashing and growling as they forced their way across the terrain.

Had the greater battle already begun? Would it matter whether they succeeded here or not? Elsie didn't have much hope for success. Months ago, when she'd been picking dragons off in the marsh, the groups had been small, with the hunters outnumbering them. They'd never have dared to attack an equal force, never mind one twice their size or more.

"Remember," she said in a hushed yet fierce tone, "they can smell your fear, so don't give them any. Give them anything but your fear. And remember that for all their strength and speed, their skin can still be pierced, their bodies beaten under that armor. Bog bears, black horn crabs, dire wolves, cusith, blood hawks – every beast we face can die, and dragons die the same."

She wasn't quite sure where such words had sprung from, but she was pleased with them. A grim muttering of assent and dozens of determined faces let her know the words had struck a chord.

"They're also too eager for a fight once their blood is up," she went on. "Let them make the mistakes. Now spread out, stay low, and wait for the signal."

Fifty-six leathery ghosts vanished into the foliage.

In what felt like mere heartbeats, the first red-plumed helmet came into view, then came another. Painted on their shields was that strange yellow symbol again – a mark related to the Guardian, but she knew no more than that.

With the battle now at hand, a strange and sudden ease swept over Elsie. Whatever the outcome now, it would surely be over. If she lived, she'd be back with Aleck before the moon turned. If she died, she'd see Roy again.

Quiver, feathers, string.

See Roy again?

She chided herself. How morbid and mawkish. She would live. She would go home. She'd bring a dragon helmet back for Aleck, one of those red-plumed ones. A vision came of an Aleck-like boy beside her loosing arrows at a golden helmet under a clear sky.

And on that more encouraging thought, Elsie raised the whistle to her lips.

She blew long.

She blew hard.

Fifty-six strings clapped in answer, and as many arrows hissed. Iron screeched against steel, clanged like bells, and then came the cries of pain and bellows of defiance.

"Bog devils!" a dragon roared, then they all roared it.

Elsie nocked an arrow of her own, aimed, loosed, and ducked behind cover again. Her shoulder twinged, but she pushed it aside and readied another arrow. She lunged out on the other side of her cover, aimed over the rim of a thick yellow shield, shot, then ducked down again.

Keeping low, Elsie dashed to another position – to stay in one place was death – but her foot slipped on a wet bank, and she nearly went down. She glanced for a marker to warn against dangerous pools, only to remember they hadn't had time to survey the land.

Other hunters leaped by as they darted for the cover offered by a towering wall of sawgrass, and Elsie made for it as well. Crouched again, she ground her teeth against the burn forming in her shoulder.

Arrows hissed all around.

Keeping low, Elsie lunged sideways, her bow angled flat, discovered the dragons were closer than she'd thought, and pulled back at once. Humans screamed. Then, from close overhead, there came a hollow ring of cutting steel, and long stems of sawgrass fluttered down.

Elsie dropped flat and lay as still as a board as two pairs of feet stomped through the midst of the foliage. One dragon tackled a hunter in a blur of gold and pulverized the man's face with a strong fist. The other clobbered on, swiping at every leaf or reed that might offer cover.

Fearing her heart might explode, Elsie scrambled up onto a shaky leg, just enough to get a shot off in deadly range at the dragon with the bloody fist. Her arrow punched him in turn, right through his thick neck.

Even before the dragon fell, she was off again, darting away, putting as much distance between herself and the roaring and grunting as she could. A cluster of shrill, confused, and frightened screams drew her one way, and she came upon hunters and dragons alike struggling through the black and writhing waters of a wide lagoon.

No, it wasn't the water that was writing, she realized horribly as eight black-horned crabs rose on their armored legs, their claws larger than shears. The fighting had disturbed a nest. Another high price for not being prepared.

Two of the crabs had a hunter pinned down and snapped at his leg, severing the limb. As the man went howling backward, Elsie managed to put an arrow between his eyes, sparing him a slower death as a horn crab's meal.

The dragons fared better in their armor and cleaved through the crabs' hardened shells, but they were knee-high in reeds and water and vulnerable to Elsie's keen aim. She had to scream to manage the pain in her shoulder, but she hit her mark. Her arrow took the dragon through his visor, and he fell dead. A horned crab grabbed his foot and began dragging the body into the lagoon.

Having given herself away, Elsie dashed on. She ran longer than she needed to and finally took cover again behind a domineering mangrove tree.

Her sides burned now as well, and her legs felt like they were about to fall off. She tried to draw another arrow, but her shoulder exploded in such protest that she gasped and dropped the arrow.

By now, fewer arrows were hissing and more humans were screaming. Maybe more crab nests had been trampled, or worse, a bog bear's watery den. Then came another scream – this time a woman's – over and over and over again. A gut wound, perhaps, or maybe she was being eaten alive.

Bile rose in Elsie's throat. This was her fault. She'd made this call. She'd led them here. Struggling for breath, she slumped against the tangled roots of the mangrove. Her head burned, so she ripped off the cap, and even the swamp air felt cool around her ears.

Two dragons crashed out of the marsh ahead of her, but unlike before, she couldn't hope they wouldn't notice her. Her heavy breaths and involuntary moans of pain gave the game away. They turned, saw her plain as day, then came splashing through the shallows, swords raised, faces contorted from bloodlust.

Would anyone be left to remember the attempt the Cairlav hunters had made? Likely not. No one knew where they were, and if their bodies were found, they'd likely never know the why. At best, they had blunted the edge of this flanking force, so it might not be the cause of the army's defeat. Or it might just delay that defeat by a minute or so.

Either way, Elsie was done.

She switched hands, drawing back an arrow with her left. The shot would certainly go awry, but she'd try – she'd wait until the dragons were right on top of her.

Then a new cry echoed across the marsh. A sharp howl, wolf-like but melancholy. The dragons advancing on her paused and looked around.

Of course, she thought, *this lot have never heard the cusith before.*

Elsie supposed the hounds couldn't pass up so much free meat. She willed the dragons to reach her and finish her off before the third howl rang.

She didn't want to die frozen in fear.

Dozens of emerald eyes twinkled in the tall grass, and then five slimy hounds crept into view.

Elsie couldn't hold her draw any longer. She loosed, and the arrow pinged harmlessly off a curved breastplate, yet rather than finish her, the dragons stood back-to-back, circling slowly as the cusith padded closer.

Something snarled directly above her. Elsie looked up. A white-tailed alpha stood braced on the roots of the mangrove, its hot breath washing over her face, but its focus was entirely upon the two dragons below.

Far away, more cusith howled. Then, as if waiting for a signal, the alpha above Elsie leaped at the two dragons, and his four companions pounced to assist. One dragon was sent onto his back. The other put up a longer fight, gutting a cusith, but, outnumbered, he soon fell, the hounds biting at his hands and neck. Another tore his helmet off and then went for the face.

Elsie found she was frozen in place, though this time from shock rather than fear.

Once both dragons stopped squirming, the three surviving lesser hounds ran on, but the alpha turned back to gaze at her. Elsie gazed back. Deep in its glowing eyes, she saw something new for the cusith, something like an understanding.

'Are you going to help?' the look seemed to say.

Wincing, Elsie scrambled back to her feet. The alpha barked – a wet, ethereal crack – before it hurried after its pack.

More barks and more screaming came, though this time, it was dragons. Elsie followed the hounds, blowing on her whistle, trying to find survivors. A few hunters found her quickly, then a few more joined her, and they gathered into a group of nine to sweep behind the cusith, finishing some dragons off or else dazing them with arrow fire to make them easier prey for the hounds.

More cusith issued from the reeds with hunters running at their sides, and the dragons began to flee before the combined wrath of the marshlands. Hundreds of barks and howls echoed for miles around.

The cusith's howls were different now, not melancholy but high, victorious against the common foe and invader.

For today, at least, man and hound would hunt together.

9

THE CAPTAIN

After the great hunt ended, the hunters and cusith were left in an uneasy standoff. Surrounded by countless hounds, feeling utterly exhausted and her shoulder unable to bear another shot, Elsie lowered her bow to the grass, and the survivors did the same.

Some tense heartbeats later, the cusith alphas trotted out, white tails held taut behind them, then each lowered their snouts to brush the mud. After that, the hounds dispersed, rushing back into the landscape in long trails like green rivers.

Until next time, Elsie thought, slowly retrieving her bow. It took time to count the survivors and confirm the dead. Of their fifty-six bows, twenty-three strings had been torn from the world. A heavy price, even with the unlikely victory. She wondered whether more cusith had gone to assist the main host in the greater battle.

Well, we'll discover their fate soon enough.

Before the trudge back, Elsie made sure to grab a dragon helmet from a shallow pool. Its red plume was filthy and ruffled, but both it and the gold-tinted steel might be cleaned. Trophy in hand, she led the others south toward the island.

When they arrived, the sun burned orange and low in the west, setting the loch ablaze. Already there were crows cawing. The battle was over, and it turned out they had won.

Dronithir came to find her.

"It was hard-won and too close for comfort," he said. "One slip, and we would have fallen. By saving our flank, you may well have saved the day."

Elsie had her doubts. She reckoned Dronithir had done more by defeating Norbanus in single combat, though she appreciated the words all the same.

"Without the hounds, we'd be dead," she admitted.

"Then I owe those creatures my thanks as well."

His voice shook a little, and though he tried to hide it, Elsie noticed his arm trembled too. It was the arm in which he held his magic sword in a white-knuckled grip. Despite the end of the fight, he still had it drawn, and his breathing came harder than it ought to.

"Were it that I could take those hounds across the sea and train them to bark when the Light Bearers lie."

A smile played at the corner of his lips, a slight one that diminished his handsome features. Elsie stood there, unsure, and again she felt an unsettling creep slide coldly up her neck.

"Alas not, I fear," Dronithir said with forced humor. "I doubt they'd stand the heat."

Elsie forced a weak smile in turn. "Is it really over, then?"

He nodded. "I've already taken oaths of fealty from the regular legionaries in Norbanus's host. I've ordered them to make ready to return home."

Elsie nodded in acknowledgment.

"And Norbanus is secure," Dronithir went on, waving carelessly toward where a ring of his dragons stood shoulder to shoulder, facing inward. "He's bereft of his blade, for now at least. Would you like to see him?"

"No," Elsie said, quick and hard. On that, she was sure. She just wanted to go home, but what she said was, "I need to rest. My shoulder... will you excuse me?"

"Of course. Rest up, human." Sword still in hand, Dronithir trudged off.

Elsie slinked over to the battered remnants of the human lines. When she saw old Balliol, she was surprised at how pleased she was to see him.

"You're a hard man to kill, Marshal."

He raised a finger, then hawked a gob of bloody spit. "Not for lack of them trying." One of his lower front teeth was missing. "Seems yer hard to kill an' all, lass."

Just then, her shoulder and arm pained her worse than ever. Wincing, she pressed her left fist into the meat of the joint, which eased it a bit.

"I might have gone on my last hunt."

"Aye? Well, t'was a ruddy good one, I reckon."

As he eyed the helmet under her arm, Elsie held it up for him.

"How high a bounty will you give for one of these?"

He took a moment, then barked a laugh. "More than Lord Heath will be willing tae part with, I'll wager. You can help me try to convince him, though."

"I look forward to that," she said without enthusiasm.

That night was a solemn one. Even the midges seemed to be respectful and left them well alone. When morning came, Elsie found Dronithir standing head bowed upon the battlefield. He'd plunged his sword into the ground, as if for support, and still gripped it with both hands.

"Dawn shine upon you, huntress," he said without raising his head. "Did you rest well?"

Her shoulder still ached, and there was a pounding behind her eyes, but she said, "Well enough. Did you rest at all?"

Dronithir didn't answer.

"I'm going to make this right. I'm going to ensure justice for your people... and for her."

For once, Elsie did not nod. Years ago, a young mother had begged Elsie to hunt down a cusith that had stolen her babe in the night. The mother had sought justice, but it felt like revenge. Elsie wondered whether it was justice or revenge Dronithir sought. Squint, she thought, and they could look the same.

Elsie had answered that mother's call, and she'd tried her best to kill Dronithir in the recent past. If she'd managed to exact her revenge, humanity would almost certainly have been doomed. The thought made her feel queasy. She didn't feel like hunting anymore.

"I'd take peace above anything," she said.

Dronithir met her eye then. "I mean it. I'll make them change. I'll take steps to ensure this cannot happen again. I promise."

Elsie looked into his eyes. The hardness had returned, tougher than ever.

She had no notion of what the Prince might attempt to do east across the sea, but her instincts told her he wouldn't accept compromise.

"I hope you succeed—"

She almost said his name, but something made her hesitate. To excuse it, she offered her hand again by way of parting. It took the Prince a few moments to register what she was waiting for, and once he did, he seemed to find it hard to let go of his sword. When he did let go, it was with his off-hand, and his squeeze lacked the same strength. His main hand remained around the grip as though welded in place.

She left the Prince standing on the battlefield.

Over the following days, she had the hunters shadow the dragons as they marched back to the coast and made sure they returned to their ships. Thankfully, they did just that, and once the last of their galleys vanished beyond the horizon, the beleaguered hunters from the Dales, Boreacs, Crescent, Hinterlands, and the Cairlav Marshes, along with all the soldiers, could at last return to

their homes. All of Elsie's thoughts began to turn to the little boy
in the crannog out from Torridon's shore.

The return journey through the marshlands was a quiet one.
Soldiers peeled off in groups toward their homes while the men
from the Golden Crescent and western marshes carried on past
Torridon, hugging the southern shores of Loch Minian where the
air and land were clearer.

As captain, Elsie really ought to have made her way to the
Cairlav Lodge, another crannog a day's walk west from Torridon.
But that could happen in good time. If it had to at all. She'd sooner
hang her bow than be parted from Aleck any longer, and with her
shoulder as it was, she thought she'd do better to pass the
captaincy along as soon as things were settled. Thus, when she
came within sight of Torridon's palisade walls, she ordered the
remaining Cairlav hunters to the lodge, telling them she would
follow soon.

When she, Balliol, and the local men returned through the
town gates, little seemed to have changed. The smokehouses
billowed their fishy fumes, yet a few chimneys were cold now, and
more windows were darkened. On that day, the sky was charcoal
gray, and drizzling rain dampened the mood. Yet Elsie couldn't
help but beam as she moved through the streets, dragon helmet in
hand, heading to the shore of the loch and onto the crannog's
bridge, toward the door of the Heath family home.

It swung open without her needing to knock.

A servant she didn't recognize with a haughty northern accent
decreed, "Lord Heath will be with you shortly. He asks that you
wait without—"

But Elsie hurried past him, near-sprinting through the long
curving corridors to Aleck's room. She found him asleep in his cot.
At least, she assumed it was him. He was much bigger now, of

course, with chestnut hair on his head. The Heath crannog crest was stitched upon his clothing.

After so long dreaming of this moment, she now found herself unsure what to do. She just stood there, feeling dumb and awkward and in the way. Should she wake him? She desperately wanted to wake him and hear him laugh. But she knew she shouldn't, and something about reaching out for him felt *wrong*, as though she, of all people, lacked permission.

"Elsie!" someone hissed like an angry goose. It turned out to be Lady Heath, bustling into the room and shooing her away from the cot. "What are you doing, girl? You'll wake him."

Elsie was taken aback. Somehow, she hadn't heard Lady Heath approaching.

"I... I..."

But Elsie struggled to speak. Inwardly, she cursed herself. She'd fought dragons and won. What was so difficult about this?

Aleck stirred. He opened his big blue eyes and yawned, then looked between both women. He tilted his head quizzically at Elsie, then fumbled around, gripped the posts of his cot, and pulled himself up to stand.

So she'd missed that first moment already.

Elsie couldn't take it anymore. She dropped the helmet, letting it clatter to the floor, and started forward, intending to pull Aleck out of the cot, hold him close, and never let go—

But Aleck cried out and fell back, hands flailing in front of him. He began to wail, his face puffing red and his eyes bulging in fright. Elsie froze mid-stride. Her son quickly averted his eyes from her.

Because he doesn't know me.

Aleck reached his stubby arms for Lady Heath. She picked him up, and relief broke across Aleck's face like sunshine after a storm.

"Mamma," he squeaked, burying his face into Lady Heath's shoulder.

Elsie lost time, and then her back hit the wall.

Another voice spoke low from the doorway.

"Elsie," Lord Heath said. She did not turn. "Elsie, come with me. Come on now."

What happened next was a blur. Heath's words sounded slow to her, as though passing through honey. They burned as though branded on her skin.

Heath had used the war and lack of travel to the capital to pass Aleck off as his own child. As far as the great houses were concerned, he was a late miracle bestowed upon his wife, tragically timed with Roy's death. The nobility had bought the story. So that would be that. And it would be far better for Aleck to grow up without any stink of scandal or impropriety around him. Far better for the family, too.

Elsie... Well, Elsie didn't fit into that happy tale.

Heath's final gruff apology was accompanied by a bag of gold thrust into her arms. Elsie let the bag fall with a dull thud. She couldn't think. All she registered was Aleck's wails a few doors down. She tried to go to him, but wide-shouldered guards cut her off. Rough hands took her. One clamped down on her bad shoulder, and colors popped in her vision from the pain. Struggling, crying, she fought back, but there wasn't the strength in her arm, and her feet left the floor as the guards lifted her and removed her bodily from the crannog.

They set her down upon the bridge, and the moment her feet touched wood, she pivoted and lunged, eyes set on the crannog's shut door. The guards seized her and threw her off. She tried again. And again. Seeing red, she drew her knife and received a bash to her stomach from the boss of a shield. She crumpled this time, dropping her blade. Hacking for breath, she tried reaching for her knife, but a booted foot flicked it away and into the loch.

"What's the meanin' o' this?!"

It was Balliol, though he sounded far away.

Someone hauled Elsie to her feet, then moved in front of her as more guards stomped forward.

"What do you think yer doing... Orders? Bugger that, you thick-skulled—"

Elsie staggered backward, then turned. She hadn't run on any hunt, she hadn't run from the valley, but she ran now.

"Elsie?" Balliol called. "Elsie!"

She ran and ran until her legs burned. Before she knew it, she was out of town and scrambling through the reeds, slipping thrice, the third time into a deep pool. She crawled onto a mound, hands squelching through mossy earth, and remained on all fours, panting, dripping, and soaked through her leathers. A chill all over caused her to shudder.

At some point, she got up and started moving again, heading west toward the lodge, perhaps. She wasn't sure, but the marshes soon started to spin along with her head, and she couldn't have found her way, even if the sun hadn't been swallowed by the clouds.

Rage and grief struggled for dominance. It only caused the world to spin faster.

Her hand moved in her old routine.

Quiver, feather—

But there were no feathers. She hadn't filled her quiver needlessly.

The recent months began flashing by in her head, as though her mind were flying back to when things made sense. The Prince stood bitter and ethereal, then turned younger and confident; Captain Luna lay dead between a knot of trees, then sat across a tavern table from her, exchanging hunting stories over sour ale; Elsha looked at her with bright eyes, and she did not change; Roy kissed her farewell upon the dock before morphing into the young man rowing them both far out onto the loch to be alone. And Aleck. Aleck was laid fresh and red-faced into her arms, and seeing him, hearing him, feeling him, the exhaustion of his birth left her in a rush of euphoria.

She wished to sit with that feeling forever.

Then her foot went out from under her. Mud and grass rushed up, and then she knew no more.

Darkness swirled around her like a blanket. Waterfowl squawked, though she couldn't place their cries. She heard the tall grass swaying and felt a cooling patter of rain against the back of her head. She didn't open her eyes. She wasn't sure if she could. Or if she wanted to.

Something larger and heavier parted the reeds and splattered closer to her. She thought it was a cusith, but then a hand gently shook her.

"Captain?" The man sounded concerned. "I've found her! Here!"

Whistling came next, and other whistles answered.

Part of her resisted the shaking, not wishing to leave the blanketing dark, but gentle hands turned her over, and as she rolled onto her back, a gray light forced its way through her eyelids. She blinked, first from waking and then from the pitter-patter of rain.

The hunter kneeling over her was a young marshland man. Meron. Yes, that was his name. She tried to say his name, but her dry throat and drier mouth failed to produce the sound.

More hunters emerged. One handed a large waterskin to Meron, who lowered it to Elsie's lips. She drank a little, but her stomach cramped and she turned aside, spluttering the remaining water from her mouth.

After that, someone helped her sit upright. Her shoulder ached worse than ever, and she could feel dried mud on her face.

"Where is she?" a familiar gruff voice said. Elsie looked around to see Marshal Balliol joining the gathering. He unfastened his heavy black cloak, then bent with a groan to wrap it around her shoulders. "You gave us a fright, lass."

Elsie gulped, then managed to say hoarsely, "How long have I been out here?"

"Thick end o' two days." His black eyes shone with concern, making her feel ashamed for falling to pieces. Her head thumped as though she'd been in her cups, and she placed a hand against her temple.

"I'm sorry."

"Don't be daft. You've nothin' tae be sorry for." He glanced around. "Where's yer bow?"

Elsie looked around. "I don't know."

"I'll go," someone said.

Elsie only realized she'd been staring into the middle distance when Balliol snapped his fingers loudly before her. She started, then looked at him.

"We're going to move you," he said. "We can carry you if—"

"No... I'll stand."

Somehow, she managed it. Somehow, she managed to make it to the warm lodge out on the loch and get into dry clothes. Somehow, her heart kept beating, and it pumped increasingly hot blood back through her veins. Between that and the hearth, she began to feel human again.

Days later, Elise remained sitting by the common room fire with only the mounted head of a cusith alpha above the fireplace for company. She didn't like to look at it, for the hound seemed to look upon her knowingly, accusingly. Instead, she sunk lower in the squat chair and picked at the crumbs of a dark loaf and wedge of white cheese.

A knot of anxiety still plagued her stomach, so crumbs were about all she could manage. Otherwise, her fingers played endlessly with the blue swaddling suit she'd held onto through everything. She wouldn't give that up. They'd have to prise it from her corpse if they wanted to take it as well.

Late that morning, Balliol came to join her, sinking into one of the sagging chairs by the fire. Mercifully, he didn't try telling her that things would turn out for the best. He didn't say anything, in fact. He just sat there, and that was enough until she felt ready to speak.

"You've been very kind to me. I would never have expected it. You seemed rather against me at first."

He shuffled uneasily in his chair. "Ack, I..." He exhaled hard. "Let's just say this last year has reminded me there's worse out there than a great lord's scandal. Guess a war can do that. And frankly, I don't much like what Heath has done."

"Should you speak ill of your lord?"

He shrugged. "You deserved better than that, lass. And I let him know as much. If he'd seen the half of what you did for him... for all of us—"

"Not just me, Marshal. You went far beyond your own duty."

Balliol gave a breathy laugh. "Not Marshal anymore... not after I spoke me mind like that." He held up a hand to stay her surprise. "It's nae bother. I did me bit for my grandweans, and that's enough for me. Besides, I was gettin' a bit long in the tooth for being Marshal."

Elsie made a trembling smile, and then they both gazed into the red depths of the crackling fire. They seemed to sit there for a long time, and only when a log fully blackened and snapped was Elsie shaken from her reverie.

"So, what now?" she asked. It seemed to go without saying that she wouldn't remain captain. If Heath didn't have the guts to do it, she'd leave on her own terms.

"Now that's a question," Balliol said, but he didn't offer an answer.

There was a long silence again, broken only by the popping of the fire.

Then came the thudding of someone running through the lodge, and moments later, a hunter emerged breathless into the common room.

"Captain!"

Elsie faced the hunter, her neck protesting at the movement. "Yes?"

"There's a chevalier here to see you."

"A chevalier?" she said slowly, as though the word were in another tongue. "For me?"

"Asked for you by name, Captain."

Balliol exclaimed in his own manner. "They lost?"

"No, sir – I don't think so, sir," the hunter stammered. "What should I tell him?"

"Tell him I'm coming," Elsie said. She pushed herself to her feet, swaying a little upon numb legs. Chevaliers were the cream of the Brevian mounted knights, the most elite of the highborn. Heavy cavalry weren't known to frequent the marshes.

Elsie made her way through the lodge, and Balliol followed. Outside, Elsie blinked against the unexpectedly bright day. The usual gray clouds had been burned away, and the loch sparkled.

Among the hunters and dockhands of the crannog lodge, the chevalier stood out much like a dragon, only this man's armor was silver-steel, not gold. He stood on a dry patch some way in from the shore, patting the nose of a mighty war horse adorned in a rich, quilted caparison. A wide, low-set barge tied at the closest pier informed Elsie how the knight had arrived.

"Ah," the chevalier said haughtily. "Huntress Elsie, I presume?"

She raised an eyebrow. "That's me."

"Our noble king requests your presence in Brevia at once. Hunters have proven useful in the recent war, and the more formal organization and integration of your profession is now seen as eminently favorable to humanity."

"We've been *useful*?"

"Indeed," the chevalier said, clearly not registering her tone. "Your name in particular has repeatedly reached His Majesty's ear. He is assured that you will be vital in guiding the foundations of a kingdom-wide institution. Lord Heath has already been informed."

"Has he?"

"Indeed," he repeated crisply, seeming pleased Elsie was following so well.

They were interrupted by the arrival of a young huntress in training who hadn't earned her leathers carrying a pail of oats. The knight thanked her carelessly, placed the pail before his horse, lovingly patted his steed, and then looked at Elsie expectantly again. When she didn't speak, he said, "You'll be in shock with the honor, I'm sure. Take a little time, but please make ready to leave as soon as you're able. It's a long barge trip then ride back to the capital."

Elsie was in a form of shock alright. She turned her back to the knight and went to Balliol. The old ex-marshal was scratching at his graying beard.

"Should I offer congratulations or condolences?" he asked in a low voice.

"Whichever you like. Will you come with me?"

"With you?"

"You know what you're about, and I'll be in over my head."

"To Brevia?" he asked, still stuck on the first point. "Folk there say one thing, mean two other things, and get pissy when you can't figure it out."

"All the more reason I'd like to have someone I trust with me."

"I don't... I can't—"

"I don't care what the Prince said; I can't help but feel the dragons will return. I don't want Aleck to go the same way as Roy..."

Elsie knew the King had to be made to understand what was needed to fight the dragons, should they return. But even as she envisioned speaking to a shadowy figure wearing a crown, the mother in her asserted herself again. The guilt came racing back – she couldn't leave. Yet she subdued that part more easily than before. At the battle in the mountains, she'd dreamed of stealing her son back and fleeing with him. That would be her only option now, but Aleck would be far better off raised as a lordling than experiencing the pitiful, fearful life she might provide on the run.

And if I go far away, Aleck can grow up in peace. There'll be fewer whispers behind his back. He'll live a better life.

"I can do more good for him this way," Elsie said. "We can do a lot to make your grandweans safer, too."

Balliol sighed, but in the depths of his eyes, a new energy twinkled. "Aye, right enough. Aye, alright, I'll come with you, lass."

Elsie went to tell the chevalier the good news. "I'll come."

"Jolly good!" The knight beamed. "The journey has been long, so I should like some rest before setting off again. Settle what affairs you must, and so forth. Bethany and I shall await you on the morrow at first light."

"Bethany?" Elsie asked.

The chevalier patted his steed proudly.

Elsie nodded, and despite herself, she had to suppress a smile. Roy had told her stories about what the chevaliers could be like, but it was another thing entirely to experience it. Perhaps the capital would be more amusing than she'd thought.

The next morning, Elsie returned to the docks dressed in a new set of mud-red and green leathers, with a quiver full of arrows, a new dark treated bow, and old Balliol walking by her side. He wore his breastplate again, only now he didn't strain to breathe in it – in fact, he wore it well. The months of toil had hardened him again as they had hardened her. He didn't say much, which she appreciated. A huntress grew accustomed to quiet, and no doubt there would be plenty of noise in Brevia to contend with.

The chevalier and Bethany were already aboard the low barge, and the bargeman was ready to depart.

"Good morrow, huntress. Are you ready?"

A twinge shot through Elsie's shoulder, but she managed to run her hand through the old routine.

Quiver, feathers, string, and now her heart, touching the spot where she'd sewn Aleck's blue swaddling suit to the underside of her leathers.

"We're ready," she said, stepping aboard.

Balliol grunted. "Is this a bad time tae mention I cannae swim?"

Elsie offered him her hand. He took it, and once aboard, she sat cross-legged on the deck with him so he wouldn't feel out of place.

"Homeward, bargeman," the knight called. "May your pole and these waters speed us smoothly on our way!"

"Eyes wide and ahead," Elsie muttered. Aleck, Roy, and the war lay behind. The unknown spread open before her. "Eyes wide and ahead."

The bargeman plunged his pole into the shallow water, and the barge began to drift out onto the loch. Balliol closed his eyes and placed a steadying hand on the baggage, leaving Elsie alone to contend with the chevalier.

"So, huntress, tell me of the war. The stories that have reached Brevia sound more fantasy than fact. Magic swords and lost loves, noble princes and heroic sacrifices, and other such things the small folk are fond of. Next, they'll be saying the fairies whizzed out of Val'tarra with silver branches to smite the dragons and turn them back to lizards." He chortled. "But you were involved. You can set the story straight for me."

Involved? she thought. That was one way of putting it. Yet next to dragon princes, swords from the gods, and a battlefield duel between dragon lords, her own role seemed small, even to her.

"Well, huntress?" the knight said, impatient.

"Call me captain if you please, ser knight. Captain Elsie—"

And here her next words sprang to her mind as if from nowhere.

"Captain Elsie the Green."

AFTERWORD

Hello again! What did you think of Elsie's tale? I'm much happier with this new version of it.

I'd like to chat about the process of this rewrite and offer some of my thoughts on the story. In doing so, I'm going to assume you've read the main trilogy, so if you haven't read it yet, stop right now and come back later. There are spoilers ahead!

gets megaphone SPOILERS AHEAD!!!

Alright, so if you're still here, I assume you've read the main trilogy AND now *The Huntress* and care enough to know my thoughts on a few things.

Excellent!

Revisiting *The Huntress* was a very interesting exercise. At first, I felt lost, drowning in a sea of hazy memories about *Dragon's Blade* and its lore, canon, and style. But after just a few days of working on it, I was surprised by how much knowledge rushed back to me.

In many ways, the scope of *The Huntress* would fill a full book if I let it spin out in all the ways it might. For instance, there's no mention of the human wizards and witches who form the Cascade Conclave. Just what the heck were they doing during these existential times? Were they even around? The main trilogy doesn't make it clear, and I never made definitive timeline notes this far back in the history of Tenalp. Given that not a single character thinks about or mentions wizards in the novella, I have to conclude that the Conclave doesn't exist at this time. Their creation might well be one of the measures introduced by Dronithir when he becomes the Dragon King. Asking the fairies to teach humans the ways of magic would give them powerful casters with which to deter future dragon aggression.

There is another option, however, which is that the Conclave did exist in this period but didn't take part, given their need to refrain from heavy use of magic. As the historian Tiviar mentions:

"The wizards and witches of the Cascade Conclave are simultaneously remarkable and worth little attention. Their use of magic is extraordinary, but their reserved nature – a necessity in handling magic in such a free manner – has dissuaded them from engaging in major events of the world. Had the order joined one war or another in full force, the course of history could well have been different." (Veiled Intentions, Dragon's Blade #2, Chp 10)

To create some headcanon, I think the former option works best. It lends weight to Dronithir's desire to prevent further warfare, but, like his other ideas, the Conclave didn't pan out as intended, given their aversion to engaging in major events. Like the creation of the Bastion, it would have been taken with the right intentions but wouldn't achieve the desired effect.

Dronithir ain't perfect. But more on him later.

Another question is just what the heck did the fairies think of this war? Ostensibly, Norbanus seemed on the warpath to wipe humanity out – would the fairies have just let that happen? Once again, I'm not fully sure what they thought. The events of this war with Dronithir and Norbanus were mentioned in the main series as core human-dragon history, but the fairies never seemed to play a role. I think that's a consequence of *Dragon's Blade* being my first series in which I didn't fully consider all avenues like this.

I have to believe they would have done something. They don't seem the sort to just watch mass murder. If we wanted to be generous, we could imagine the fairies hotly debating what to do in the background and perhaps marshaling a force to assist humanity by the time the Battle of the Bogs occurs.

Significant changes have been made to Dronithir in this update. In the original novelette, Dronithir was painted as much too virtuous. Upon re-examining the story six years later, I realized my subconscious had been chasing something good, but whether from rushing or lack of experience, I didn't quite click onto it the first time around. Tiviar, the great historian, likes to question events and wonders what the truth is. If I'm going to portray Dronithir – 'humanity's greatest friend' – I think it behooves the tone of the trilogy to show things weren't quite what the legend suggests. The Prince did indeed save humanity, of that there is no doubt. He did fall in love with a human girl and was devastated by her loss. But was it grief at her loss that triggered the gods to present him with the Champion's Blade, or was it something else? That I'll leave for you to ponder, though if you've read the main series, you probably know the answer.

This revision also gave me a chance to better contrast Dronithir against another dragon prince turned king – Darnuir. The whole point of Darnuir's arc is one of redemption, from someone who yearned for power (ostensibly to do good) to one who actually did have all the power in the world but willingly chose to give it up. Dronithir too gained great power, and he really intended to make it harder for dragons to wage war against humanity – hence why he ordered the construction of the Bastion (and possibly set up the Cascade Conclave, as I suggest above). Dronithir realized that the institution of the Guardians had become too powerful and susceptible to bad ideas. He set out with the intent to reform, not destroy, as he is a believer himself – after all, he encountered the gods in a tangible way. But he suffered one fatal flaw. In his heart, he sought revenge.

When Dronithir gained power, his dark desire was to hurt Norbanus in turn and break the Guardian's power. It wasn't honest, truthful, or forthrightly done. At some point, the Champion's Blade must have left him, for he never wielded the Dragon's Blade alongside it. In the end, he failed. We see the results of that echo centuries later into the main series.

In short, Dronithir held on to bitterness, and Darnuir managed to let it go.

Feel free to disagree if you like! Death of the author and all that...

Whatever you think, and however you feel, thank you for reading my rambling thoughts. I think the novella now complements the main series well, and for me, it turned out to be a satisfying return to the world of *Dragon's Blade*.

If you aren't aware, the entire trilogy is now available in one giant 1,100-page hardback omnibus. The cover art from Chris McGrath looks stunning on such a thick scale. If you enjoyed the trilogy as an ebook collection or as the 46-hour audiobook, perhaps you'd like to get an omnibus for your shelf.

Last but far from least, some thanks are in order! Big thanks to author Alec Hutson for his editorial input on both novellas and to Anthony Wright for his fantastic copy-editing. A huge thank you to Dave Cruse, who agreed to return to the world of *Dragon's Blade* to narrate Elsie's story. And a special thank you goes to authors J.A. Andrews, Virginia McClain, and J. Patricia Anderson for their feedback and insights on Elsie as a mother.

Next up on my to-do list is Songs of Chaos #4. That'll be another whopper of a book, so I'd best get to work – I'll see you there to continue Holt and Ash's perilous adventures.

Before signing off, I'd like to ask you to consider the usual things.

Please Review!

Firstly, if you haven't already done so, please consider leaving a review for *The Dragon's Blade* on Amazon, Audible, or Goodreads. It all helps immensely.

There will be a listing for *The Huntress* on Goodreads as well and eventually on Amazon etc. when the combined print edition goes live. Even though these are free novellas, please also consider reviewing both online where you can. It all helps in making the offer appealing to more readers who will then come join the community!

Recommend To Friends and Family!

If you've enjoyed my work please recommend it to any friends or family who you think would enjoy it too. Word of mouth is still the best way books find new readers.

Pick up a copy in print

If you've grabbed *Last Stand* and *The Huntress* for free on my mailing list and would like to have a copy for your shelf, you can buy a paperback or hardback edition that contains both stories in one. You'll be able to find them online in all the usual places, including signed copies from The Broken Binding.

Please note: the physical edition may not be ready right away, Keep an eye out on my socials, mailing list etc, for all updates on it.

Follow Me

Discord: https://discord.gg/C7zEJXgFSc
Instagram: @michael_r_miller_author
Facebook: https://www.facebook.com/michaelrmillerauthor
Reddit: r/MichaelRMiller
Twitter: @MMDragons_Blade

Check out the sketches!

Don't forget to have a gander at the sketches at the back of the book!

Michael R. Miller
    November 2023

As a bonus for this print edition, I'm adding in sketches I had made many years ago by artist David North. They were made to help me visualise key elements and characters.

What better way to begin than with the titular sword itself! I see the cross guard wings as being larger and wider than this, even if that wouldn't be practical from a balance perspective. The Dragon King wielding this thing doesn't play by the normal rules.

Next up we have the Guardian's Blade. The Roman inspiration is clear in this very gladius looking sword.

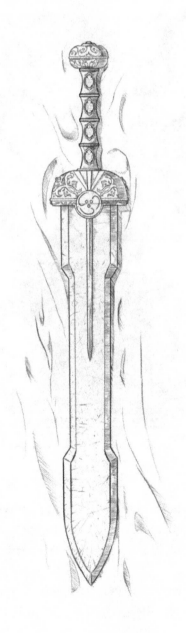

Those of you who have bought the hardback omnibus edition of the trilogy may recognise this from the title page. If you still haven't worked it out, this is our demon friend Dukoona, Lord of the Spectres.

Dukoona is the very first POV we meet in the series prologue. That prologue was actually the last part I added to book 1 during the final stages of editing back in 2015. This piece is of that first moment when he materialises at the behest of the dark lord.

As he and his kind can meld fully into shadows for safety, fast travel and to setup ambushes, I think this piece perfectly encapsulates him.

Dukoona and his Spectres help control and guide the lesser demons. These creatures are pulled into the world against their will. Their true form is unknown. This horrific skeletal and shadow form is the result of them being ripped from whatever world they truly belong to.

They aren't the strongest or the most skilled in battle but they make up for that in vast numbers and a lack of fear. To be cut by one of their rusted shards is to risk infection from such an unclean wound. They even have poisonous residue coating their crude weapons.

Moving away from the demonic forces, this chap is a sketch of our frost troll friend, Ochnic. He takes that satchel everywhere.

A fun fact, the name Ochnic was the name of my original World of Warcraft main character. At first I played a human rogue, then my guild switched to Horde during the Burning Crusade. I re-rolled a troll rogue but kept the name Ochnic. It seemed fitting to name our trollish hero after him.

And here we have our two leading wizards. Castallan on the left, and Brackendon on the right. Note Brackendon's injured right hand from over doing it on spell work.

Time to reveal something a little embarrassing. I started

thinking of the ideas which would eventually become The Dragon's Blade very young - aged 9 or 10. Way back when, I knew I wanted two wizards, one good and one bad (see childhood obsession with LOTR) and I wanted the bad guy to control a powerful fortress our heroes would have to overcome. Struggling with a name for this evil wizard, I asked my dad for help. I explained the fortress thing and he said to call him 'Castellan' or so I assume. What I heard was 'CastAllan'... and having no idea what an actual castellan was, I assumed the 'cast' part of the name related to him casting spells...

I can't recall the moment I realized my blunder but whenever the lightbulb flicked on above my head it was already too late. The character was firmly Castallan in my head and I could not dislodge it.

Our final sketch is of the main character, Darnuir - the Reborn King. It was hard to get the design of the pauldrons right. The imagery here still smacks a little too much like a bird, I think, but it served me well to help envision his look. I believe this is supposed to be him ready to head into battle at the end of book 1.

As he's our last image and the main character it seems fitting to dedicate a full page to him.

SONGS OF CHAOS DND 5E

Wider Path Games has created a way for you to role play inside the Songs of Chaos world with their DND 5E setting! This book contains everything players and GMs need to adventure in the Songs of Chaos world, including...

- 6 new dragon rider classes where you play the role of both dragon and dragon rider
- New Power system with more than 100 Powers to choose from
- 44 monsters that bring the world to life, including a system for turning any creature into a blight-infected monster
- A system for crafting your unique dragon rider weapon
- 14 new Special Items
- 25 engaging encounters that bring to life unique aspects of the world
- An adventure that introduces players to the Songs of Chaos RPG

Wider Path have also teamed up with the company Grinning Gods to create minis to go alongside the campaign. There are 6 unique dragon figurine designs to choose from or you can get them all in one bundle.

Fire Dragon, Storm Dragon, Emerald Dragon, Ice Dragon, Lunar Dragon, and Mystic Dragon.

More info and links to all of this can be found on my website www.michaelrmiller.co.uk